PRAISE FOR *YOUR STORY, MY STORY*

"*Your Story, My Story* is a novel you cannot put down until the final page has been read . . . it's like staying up all night listening to the intimate confessions of a close friend and staggering back to your own wan existence, reeling from the intense emotional journey."

—*De Morgen*

"Connie Palmen's great achievement in *Your Story, My Story*, a beautifully written book, is that the voice of Ted Hughes wins you over from the word go. You forget that the voice is in fact Palmen's. That's when you know the novelist has done her job. Sheer class."

—*Het Parool* ★★★★

"*Your Story, My Story* is captivatingly romantic."

—*Elsevier* ★★★★★

Your Story, My Story

OTHER TITLES BY CONNIE PALMEN

The Laws

The Friendship

A Novel

Your Story, My Story

CONNIE PALMEN

TRANSLATED BY EILEEN J. STEVENS AND ANNA ASBURY

AMAZON **CROSSING**

Previously published as *Jij zegt het* by Prometheus in the Netherlands in 2015. Translated from Dutch by Eileen J. Stevens and Anna Asbury. First published in English by Amazon Crossing in 2021.

Published by Amazon Crossing, Seattle

www.apub.com

Amazon, the Amazon logo, and Amazon Crossing are trademarks of Amazon.com, Inc., or its affiliates.

ISBN-13: 9781542022408 (hardcover)
ISBN-10: 1542022401 (hardcover)

ISBN-13: 9781542004633 (paperback)
ISBN-10: 1542004632 (paperback)

Cover design by Kimberly Glyder

Printed in the United States of America

First edition

Your Story, My Story

To most people, we exist only in books, my bride and I. For the past thirty-five years, I've had to watch with impotent horror as our real lives were buried beneath a mudslide of apocryphal stories, false witness, gossip, fabrication, and myth; how our true, complex personalities were replaced by hackneyed characters, reduced to mere images, tailor-made to suit a readership with an appetite for sensationalism.

And in all of this, she was the brittle saint, I the brutal traitor.

I have remained silent.

Until now.

She had something in her of the religious fanatic, that reckless longing for a higher form of purity, the saintly and violent willingness to sacrifice herself—her old, false self—to murder it, so that she could be born again, clean, free, and, above all, real.

In the seven years we were together, I never saw her with anyone—not even our children—as she really was, the way I knew her, the woman I lived with, the woman who, stamping like a filly in heat, bit my cheek and drew blood the first time we met.

We didn't embrace—we attacked each other.

Snorting—with pleasure, with joy—I yanked the red hair band from her head, tore the silver earrings from her lobes, I would have liked to rip her dress to shreds, to strip her of all the trappings of decency, obedience, and civility, of falseness.

It was cruel. It hurt.

It was real.

We plundered each other.

Less than four months later, I married her.

I should have known that for a woman who bites instead of kisses, loving was the same as lashing out. I should have realized that by stealing her jewelry, I was only tearing away her ornamentation and taking it as my trophy. Whoever begins this kind of love knows that violence and destruction are hidden at its heart. To the death. One of us was done for from the very start.

It was either her or me.

In that all-consuming violence called love, I'd met my match.

I loved her—I've loved her ever since. If her suicide was the trap she used to catch me, to swallow me, to absorb me, to become one body, she succeeded. A bridegroom taken hostage by death, linked eternally in a posthumous marriage, as inseparable as she wanted me to be from her.

Her name is my name.

Her death is my death.

I believe in something like a real self and know how rare it is to hear it speak, to see it liberated from its cocoon of falseness and insignificance, the sham appearances we present to others to win them over, to mislead them. The more dangerous the real self, the more refined the masks. The more caustic the poison we would like to spew over others—to paralyze them, to kill them—the sweeter the nectar with which we lure them toward us, to be near us, to love us.

She was a sweet-smelling barrel of venom.

I'd never before met anyone for whom love and hate were so close that they were practically the same. She wanted more than anything else to love somebody, but when she actually did, she hated it. She wanted more than anything to be adored, but she mercilessly punished anyone who ever loved her.

Hidden behind a facade of crushing cheerfulness was a shy hare with a soul of glass, a child full of fears, nightmarish amputations, imprisonments, electrocutions. And I—the amorous shaman—adored that fragile, wounded girl, her real self, and wanted to do what a lover's devotion requires: shatter her mask like a tender iconoclast. Because I loved her, it was up to me to rip her out of her shell of falseness—both as a woman and as a writer—to enable her to make her voice heard. The frightened voice, the angry voice, the maudlin voice with which she whined about trivialities, the muted voice she used to torment and humiliate, the forbidden voice like a raging fury she used to ostracize everyone who had wounded her. Her tongue of stone needed to be able to dance to the meter of her soul, that black soul of which she was justly frightened. It was up to me to raise her from that death.

What I didn't understand then was that I was also liberating myself. Her madness is my madness.

From the age of thirteen, my head was filled with myths, legends, folktales, a secret world of magical knowledge populated by cruel gods who devoured their sons, and powerful goddesses in the changing guises of virgin, mother, hag. My sister added astrology, tarot cards, and the Ouija board to the mix. By the age of twenty, I was able to work out a complete horoscope for my family and advise friends on girls they could share heaven with, or those they were better off avoiding like the plague. I looked at the position of the stars and planets every morning to see what they had to tell me.

If, on the day we met, I had listened to what they were saying—not softly whispering, but howling at the top of their lungs—I would have locked myself in my room instead of going to that night's presentation of the first—and last—issue of our poetry magazine. I would never have met her, or perhaps would have met her at another moment, a day when it wasn't written in the stars that a disastrous meeting awaited me, an explosive collision of astral energy that would change my life forever.

I am a skeptical fortune-teller: I have too little faith.

I went.

It was crowded, noisy, smoky as hell. She appeared like a long-legged goddess between the existentialist men in turtlenecks and the pasty English women with whom I was all too familiar. At the university, her fame had preceded her. I knew who she had to be, the exuberant American girl with a number of publications to her name.

A lustrously polished woman rose up before my eyes, a vision from the promised land. As soon as I touched her marble skin, I would be able to reach across the Atlantic Ocean to American literature. With her full-moon face and copper-colored, satiny complexion she looked like a Hollywood actress. A pearly smile, teeth white as a shark's, gleaming between fleshy lips painted blood red, sun-kissed blond wavy hair; everything that was reckless about her had been reined in by a close-fitting dress, red and black, the colors of Scorpio. She danced a little too wantonly, a little too brazenly, with my best friend, Lucas, as if half-entranced, but she wasn't—she wanted me to witness this display. In the brief hush in which the music of the world falls silent and nature holds its breath, gathering strength for a devastating hurricane, she took a few wobbling steps in my direction—my inebriated goddess—a pair of blackish-brown eyes feverish with the urge to mate.

I walked toward her; I called her by name.

I said, "Sylvia."

Surprised by the recognition, she had to shout to be heard above the hot-blooded jazz and boasting men, and so she did, she shouted. She barked my own lines at me like Hecate, entire stanzas from the poems she'd just read in our magazine.

A sweet, artificial aroma of lilies and spring blossoms surrounded her, but when I grabbed her and led her from the dance floor, I picked up her true odor, sharp as musk, sweetly sour as the sweat of a female deer in heat. I went into the night a marked man, with the imprint of her teeth on my cheek.

It was February 25, 1956.

I was hers.

Not four, but twenty-seven days later, our own leap day dawned, that dubious gift from the gods, the twenty-four-hour surplus needed to make the sum of eternity add up. She had just one day left before she began a trip through Europe. She gave it to me. It was the Friday that would determine my past, present, and future.

Cambridge is a village, a hotbed of gossip and backbiting. She'd found out indirectly that on two occasions, in the middle of the night, I'd stood with Lucas beneath her fourth-floor window and drunkenly bellowed her name and tossed small clumps of earth against the panes of glass—the wrong ones, we later discovered. After the failure of this clumsy Romeo act, I roped my friend into bringing her to my room in London. Lucas, who was from Tennessee and full of vicarious shame for all the American traits he saw in her—the aggressive superficiality, noisy posturing, and intrusive brazenness—begged me not to use him as a go-between in a love that was doomed, thus making him partly culpable for everything that was to come.

I didn't listen to the messenger.

He brought her to me, delivered her to 18 Rugby Street, and disappeared.

The trophies of the first day were on the low table. She came in fluttering like a bird, animated, excitable, nervous, enveloped in a unique cobalt-colored aura. She cooed my name.

She said, "Ted."

She noticed the hair band, the earrings, and—as if afraid of giving too much away by speaking my name—she added, "The black marauder." Taken with this epithet, I felt like a fairy-tale villain, but a couple of minutes later I realized that she had immortalized me in that image and was quoting herself. Heart still racing from her journey, she said that in the hours after we met, she'd written me a poem. She sat down, took out two sheets of paper crammed with writing—I caught a glimpse of her handwriting, the juvenile curves of a teenage girl—and, in an American accent, she introduced me to her image of me: a predator, a black panther pursuing her. One day she'd have her death of him, she said.

"I hope you're not clairvoyant," I joked when she was finished and suddenly looked at me timidly.

"Oh, but I am," she said in all seriousness.

I was to find hundreds of examples of her accuracy, of that uncanny ability to read other people's minds, predict events, smell danger, know at a distance what I was doing, thinking, experiencing. Having inherited the burden of the seer from my mother, I'm not frightened by this talent. It renews my feeling that I am accompanied by a guardian angel, in natural contact with the departed.

We sat opposite one another, talking, listening, discovering one surprising coincidence after another: a shared love of Yeats, Blake, Lawrence, Dostoyevsky. Her dissertation on Dostoyevsky's doppelgänger motif had earned her first-class honors, and she spoke eloquently of the demonic shadow self, our dark side, our downfall, our death. She mentioned she was now working on Racine—my Continental favorite too, of course—on passion as destiny in *Phèdre*. Before we knew it, we were taking turns to quote our favorite alexandrines—she in the role of the desperate suicide victim, Phaedra; I as the falsely accused Hippolytus—the foreshadowing of a fatal casting, even then. She squealed that she'd received her essay on *Phèdre* back three weeks ago from her favorite Cambridge lecturer and mentor, with a comment in the margin on her somewhat limited view regarding passion as destiny in this tragedy—Racine really hadn't intended the holocaust she'd read into it.

As poets we're drawn to the territories marked out and occupied by another poet's scent, so I told her she was now sitting where Dylan Thomas had once sat, getting drunk with my friend Daniel's father. She stood up, knelt, kissed the wooden floor. And I, so long the enemy of love, fell deeper and deeper with each of the twenty-four hours she granted me, fell for her, for that animated, illusive beauty, for the Massachusetts accent, for my doppelgänger. When she stood up, having knelt before the bard, to return to her hotel, I pulled her to me, lifted her up, spun her around, kissed her, felt the quivers of her intense excitement, drew the scent of musk deep into my nostrils.

"Stay," I said.

"Come with me," she said.

I went with her. It was inconceivable that we should enter her hotel room together—unmarried—so we shuffled slowly through the streets of London, intertwined, stopping at every tree and bush, kissing, talking, clutching at one another.

Time and again she stroked the mark on my cheek with which she had branded me hers, whispered that she did it, she. Comical, crowing, compelled by the covetous longing to reveal herself, she told me how twenty-seven days previously, after our first meeting, she'd gone into the night without me, tottering on the arm of a friend, and with his help scaled the college wall. The nails on the top of the wall had pierced her hands.

"You were my crucifixion," she said—beaming, laughing—as she showed me her open palms, "but my stigmata don't bleed."

In the short time in which I experienced her as a tempestuous miracle, I could have guessed the role assigned to me in the dramatic narrative of her life, but the prelude to this piece went at a tempo I couldn't match. Her eyes held me like a rabbit frozen in the headlights, her voice made me as deaf to the crashing of the cymbals as to the weeping of the stars. What still enchanted me the most was her alchemist's talent for melting down the leaden facts and pouring them like golden lava into the mold of a martyr's tale. She spoke of T. S. Eliot's play *The Cocktail Party*, and described how on top of those stakes she had felt like the crucified Celia Copplestone, who chose a way of life that would lead to death.

Since childhood I've read the world as a book full of secrets, meaningful signs, and I understand every omen of that evening as the prediction of a heavenly bond between a woman and a man who live to write: she's a poet, she's beautiful and witty, well read and wanton, talented and forbidding, brilliant and dangerous.

I listened, smiled, encouraged her—don't be afraid, tell me everything. She looked up at me, almost my height. I brushed the thick blond fringe from her face and exposed the punctuation of her primal narrative, the marks on her temples, which I had yet to find out corresponded with the exclamation mark under her right eye. Now that I had licked off the makeup, the scar shone sepia in the glow of the streetlamp. She seemed briefly caught off guard, ashamed, but the drink, king of indifference, won.

"Two and a half years ago I committed suicide," she said cheerfully, "and here I am, as good as new."

I could have said goodbye then, run from this story, fled from its writer, from the leitmotif of my character, listened to the voice warning me of the inevitable consequences, commanded by the logic of the plot, but instead I was sucked in deeper, attracted by the danger, irresistibly drawn to the siren song.

When we reached the hotel, there was no way I could let her go. It was unthinkable that we could enter the night apart. We were entwined in a restrained entanglement, and so, with me glued to her, stooping, hidden under her raincoat, she smuggled me past a sleepy receptionist into the hotel, giggling nervously like a lanky teenager.

We made love like Titans, biting and voracious. Impatiently I sought the pleasures of her magnificently smooth, supple body, coiling like a snake, so much narrower and more fragile than the moon face implied. I covered her mouth to dampen the cries with which she might betray our hiding place, and when she lay beside me exhausted, I had to blow my breath into her so she could speak again.

In the afterglow of sex, languid and distant, she told me about the death of her father when she was eight, about her mother, brother, live-in grandparents, her German background, bouts of depression, Dr. Beuscher, the rejection of a story, not being admitted to a coveted writers' workshop, that to her the desire to write was the same as the desire to live, that one didn't work without the other, that she stopped loving life when her imagination seemed dead, she had been afraid she would never get another sentence down on paper. She admitted she'd secretly hoped that the electroshock therapy would undo that paralysis, resurrect the current of numbed talent, that the engine of the imagination would kick in, that she would rise like Lazarus and write.

She said that soon after our meeting, she had decided to describe her therapy in detail, with a light touch, avoiding sentimentality, and offer the story to our magazine.

"Give it to me," I said.

She described the electrocution as a joke gone wrong, mocked the indifferent executioners who took her away like an animal to an underground room, bound her to a table with leather straps, plugged her head—her temples—into the implement of torture with a wire crown of electrodes, pulled the lever without anesthesia or warning, sent 450 volts through her brain, ripped apart her dreams, and scorched the delicate skin at her temples. With the smell of burnt flesh in my nose—my poor child, my girl—I kissed the tips of my fingers and laid them on the quotation marks of her drama. She trusted me, allowed it, closed her eyes, sighed. When she opened them again, they glistened with an old sadness, but she got hold of herself again—that wasn't where she wanted to be, she wanted to get away from the pain, back to the self-mockery she had used all her life to make everything bearable—and she told me how for a moment that morning she had thought herself reborn, resurrected from a brief death.

"Death and resurrection." She smirked. "It's something I'm exceptionally good at. You might even say I surpass God's own son."

I didn't laugh, didn't ask questions.

I stroked the scar, the next fragment of the story.

The electrocutions didn't have the desired effect. Instead of reviving the creative spirit, they silenced every voice that had ever spoken in her, dead, as if she'd never possessed a grain of imagination, as if she were like everyone else, destined for a monotonous existence as a housewife in a Boston suburb, stupid, fat, and knitting. She couldn't sleep, think, or write anymore, she couldn't live anymore. She tried to imitate the suicide of her idol Virginia Woolf by drowning herself in the ocean, but the water refused her gift and spat her out. Then it was Monday, August 24, and that day brought the beginning of another week of life with a silent head—an unbearable prospect. Like every miserable soul, she cursed Mondays, with their oppressive suggestion of hope and new opportunities. Her mother was going to the cinema that afternoon, her brother had a summer job, her grandparents were in the back garden that sunny day. She knew where her overprotective, overworked, widowed mummy had hidden a full bottle of sleeping pills, wrote a note—nothing special—with a steady hand, so as not to arouse suspicion, saying she'd gone for a long walk and would be home tomorrow. She opened the metal box, pocketed the pills, put it back where it belonged, snatched a blanket from the cupboard, filled a glass of water, and descended to the cellar—To the underworld, she thought with a grimace. The entrance to the crawl space under the house was at eye level, hidden by large pieces of firewood. She cleared the way, pulled herself up, crawled into the cave, and covered the opening by restacking the logs. Wrapped in a blanket, she shuffled as deep as she could into the cellar refuge. Half reclining, leaning on one elbow, just as the Romans lay during bacchanals, she consumed the fifty sleeping pills, her last supper. She lay down and waited for death.

"Yes, of course!" she said to me, eyes twinkling, as if in answer to a question I hadn't asked. As if I should have known what was coming.

And I knew.

"I know my classics," she said sardonically, "so yes, of course I called to him, prayed and begged and cried, 'Father, Father, why have you forsaken me?'"

Swinging between admiration and consternation—while also captivated by a delightful fear I could not name—I didn't realize that on the first night we spent together, she'd already introduced me to my greatest rival, a God the Father, omnipotently absent in death, and that it was death with whom I had to battle for her soul. And who knows, perhaps this was when I began to lose the battle.

The exclamation mark had not yet been drawn. Suddenly tired, even a little bored, she started on the final chapter of this familiar story she'd written earlier. How after three days the logs were pushed away from the entrance and she—less glorious than her illustrious role model—was pulled out, wrapped in her shroud, half-conscious, encrusted with dried vomit, adorned with worms like sticky pearls. A bloody gash gaped under her right eye, probably from sitting up in the confined space and tearing her face open on a rough stone. The failure of a final act of love made her deathly miserable.

It was only months later, after being discharged from the psychiatric clinic, that she discovered how close she had come to achieving posthumous fame at the age of twenty. Thanks to her mother's maddening overprotectiveness—and her mistrust, it has to be said, she didn't believe a word of that note—the police were called in almost immediately and informed of the bouts of depression. Her mysterious disappearance was the top story on the radio news that same evening. The next three days she appeared, photo and all, on the front pages of several local newspapers.

"Talented Smith Student Missing in Wellesley"
"Search for the Plath Girl Turns Up Nothing"
"Smith Student Found Alive in Cellar"

She lay there so warm in my arms, my resurrected goddess, that I wanted her anew, hungrily began to arouse her desire, to elicit the blissful moans, those un-English, thoroughly American sighs of pleasure. She was under me and on top of me, she scratched and scraped, and I bit and pinched, and in her, thrusting, moaning, my eyes on her contorted face, at my release let slip that other name with an *S* and an *I* and an *L*, a twist of the tongue which—in a state of reduced consciousness—erred and formed not Sylvia but Shirley. She pretended not to have heard, but in the brief seconds in which she opened her eyes and looked at me, I saw—besides the dismay—a lightning bolt of hatred.

In dawn's half-light I left her in the hotel and walked home in a daze—suddenly lonelier than I had ever felt. My friend Michael was staying at my place, so I had to knock on my own door at that early hour to get in. I knocked three times, the signal for the second floor. It was a while before he opened the window and threw the keys down. Michael, surprised by my excitement and confusion, went to the kitchen, grabbed a pan, and began to fry sausages and eggs. The only answer I could give to his curious questions was, "She's the one."

In retrospect—how many times will I have to avail myself of that ominous adverbial phrase, that sinister temporal expression of the revealing post-factum, the portentous announcement of an unmasked recollection, with its hint of regret, or its disconcerting ability to expose the passion of my twenty-five-year-old self and all his mistakes and incorrect interpretations—in retrospect, I read her journals.

I have never been able to explain to anyone how horrifying that was.

In hundreds of closely written pages, her handwritten flourishes revealing how she felt at that moment, I encountered her once again, stripped of camouflage, sorrowful, sullen, suspicious, and audacious, yet I barely recognized myself, the prisoner of a distorted perspective, misunderstood, my actions misinterpreted.

In retrospect, reading her version of the facts, often diametrically opposed to mine, robbed me of my earliest memories. I saw the innocent clumps of earth which Lucas and I had thrown at the wrong window transformed into mud, from which she concluded that we were dragging her name through the mire like that of a whore. My vision of a heavenly bond also turned out to be the one-sided view of a fool in love. In her journals I was able—compelled—to read that I was not yet the chosen one, just one of the many drooling candidates, sized up, prodded, and looked in the mouth like stallions at a horse market.

At that early hour, as I combatted my insatiable hunger with breakfast, my voice limited to the hum of that one mantra—She's the one, she's the one—she was stepping onto the ferry to the Continent, battered and bruised by love. She was starting her journey through Europe in Paris, a city she knew from a previous visit. She hadn't mentioned—hadn't admitted—that she was going to search for the man to whom she had pledged her soul, that it wasn't just a student's spring trip—the cultural imperative of every budding intellectual—but she was travelling to glue together a dismembered self, to get her soul back, or to give it to that man forever. In groveling, pleading letters to her lover, she threatened to kill her body if it had to continue without the precious soul she'd pledged to him. And with a mixture of compassion and satisfaction, I read that the concierge had let her into the Parisian apartment of the rival I did not know—will never know, who has remained enviably untraceable to all the snooping biographers and highly skilled vultures—and she found the crackling aerogrammes with their page-long pleas unopened and carelessly thrown about.

Around that hour of degradation and desolation, so harrowing to her, I must have been sitting down at my desk to write. It is not the first time in my life that—in retrospect—I have been surprised to read how prophetic it was, how much greater the insight of the poet than that of the blind man, of the sighing lover who only has to call to mind her naked, athletic body—and everything she could do with it, every sensation she could arouse in his—to burst out of his skin with excitement. The poet is the diagnostician, the healer who locates the tumor before the patient knows he is suffering from an incurable disease, even before he feels the pain that warns him of the trauma.

"Ridiculous" is the first word he writes.

That day, stubbornly contradicting the lover's howling loins, the poet writes that it's ridiculous to call it love, that her absence feels like the wound of a man shot down who looks up at her after he is hit—at the bird of one note, one cry—then dies.

"Loss" is the word with which he concludes his first poem for her.

Three weeks later she stood with a gleaming Samsonite—containing Paris, Munich, Venice, and Rome—at the door of 18 Rugby Street, where I awaited her, my sinews tense with desire. Women can smell the scent of others on their lover's skin far better than men can, so I couldn't smell them, the used-up lovers from that trip, tried out and discarded, crossed off the list of potential bridegrooms. I was under the illusion that I was the only one and—ignorant of the desperate quest to reunite the fragments of a shattered self—that's what I became that night. It was April, the month judged for all time by T. S. Eliot as the cruelest of its peers, and it was Friday the thirteenth.

How much symbolism can a story bear, how much a life?

The thirteenth of April turned out to be her father's birthday, 18 Rugby Street was to play a macabre role in the final weekend of her life, and on a future Friday the thirteenth, I would precipitate our ruin.

The days and numbers, stars and planets, warned me, as did my friends, but my happiness resembled that of my childhood, when I went into the countryside with my brother, ten years older, and we fished for days on end, hunted game, sat next to one another in silence in the evenings, or I listened to tales of Indians and ghosts, feeling so connected with another person that afterwards I was always in search of a twin bond that resembled it, a happiness so powerful that I dissolved and disappeared. The woman who reached out to that child, took him by the hand, and led him back to that lost paradise would be mine.

She was the one.

Anyone who knew her only superficially could not have suspected that there was a warrior concealed inside her, that she was more androgynous than you might have guessed from the prim and proper girl with the ponytail. She wanted someone to test her strength against, she wanted to fight, and for that she sought out the biggest, strongest man she could find.

Me.

Why do so few people understand that the disdain of others, their condemnation of the one you love, in fact strengthens your love? I could read the dismay at my choice in the eyes of everyone around me. And it wasn't just dismay; in some it was downright hatred. They disliked her. They felt betrayed by me, but they held her responsible. A band of rebels, destined for an exceptional life, which we frivolously and carelessly postponed as long as possible, we had warned one another against marriage and the power of women. The Irish, Scottish, and Celtic ballads we sang in the evenings in our rooms or in the pubs taught us to be on guard against the temptations of the weaker sex, the mysterious power of a woman to domesticate a man, to transform him into an obedient wretch. They probably blamed her for the fact that they suddenly saw me with new eyes. I, the coarse Yorkshireman, had chosen this exalted woman above all others, given my heart to a gushy, excessive creature, the prototype of pretense and artificiality, fanatical, exaggerated in all things.

Friends, like family, want you to remain unchanged, while love has the indecent capacity to transform you, to enrich you with a new take on everything you were once familiar with. The more she fell into disfavor with everyone, the more dogged my impulse to protect her from a hostile world, the more powerful my conviction that only I knew what she was really like. Only I knew the cross she bore, that the most dangerous enemy did not lie in wait behind the walls of their houses, but that she nourished him like a snake in her bosom.

I was just starting to unravel the mythology of her life and gave her permission to read mine. The myths are the artistic archive of universal human truths, discovered and written down to allow us to survive, the repository of the battle which human imagination has fought through the centuries to bind the external with an internal world. They expose the pattern of our psychological drama, reveal the fabric of our character, of our most important relationships, of the emotions that drive us. All literature stems from a wounded soul, from the spiritual exertion of the human defense mechanism to heal our pain and conquer death. The search for the highest knowledge—that of the self—brings you to a character whose prototype can be found in a hero or a coward, a god or a rebel. And sometimes we have to learn to read our myth in order to make a timely escape from the narrative cage of an ancient script, from the prescribed fate which a character appears to obey without free will.

The ground opens under you only once you learn that, to others, you're also a character from a novel or tragedy, and you discover that their assignment of roles has nothing to do with your reality, that they consult different books and characters to understand you. I've seen them emerge in all shapes and sizes, the prototypical scoundrels—Bluebeard and Lord Byron, Don Juan and Judas, the Yorkshire Ripper and Heathcliff—to lock me up in an obscure tale of passion, betrayal, revenge, and brutality.

17

She gave the deceptive impression of having nothing to hide—my garrulous American girl—because she immediately converted every noteworthy experience into an anecdote: vivid, exciting, often wittily delivered, a piece of literature polished over countless retellings for varying audiences and ready to send to a women's magazine. Accustomed as I was to the shy nature of English women, I found her as awe-inspiring as Niagara, her language irrepressibly crashing down like falling water. Whenever she was telling a story, her eyes glowed like granite, her long, apelike arms swung to the cadence of her voice. She gesticulated high and low, sped up and slowed down, tasted every syllable like a sweet delicacy before pronouncing it and giving it to the world. Because what she did was really an outpouring, and like all troubadours, she held people at arm's length with her entertaining performances, although there was nothing she would have liked more than to draw everyone closer. When I looked at her, I could always see the little girl who clasped the legs of visitors as soon as they stood up to leave, crying that she loved them.

Over time she'd so perfected the retelling of two crucial events that she'd lost all sense of their actual meaning, as if turning them into anecdotes distanced her from the experiences rather than enabling her to penetrate deeper. One was how she recklessly raced down the ski runs without knowing how to ski, fell and broke her leg; the other was a ride through Cambridge traffic on a bolting white stallion, Sam, hanging on to his neck, skimming the surface of the road. These were the two occasions when she had felt at one with herself, alive, intensely happy, ecstatic. When I suggested she must have been scared to death, unsure if she'd emerge unscathed, she said that it was the fear of death that colored the experiences and made them the happiest of her life. I still remember the tenderness of her look when she added that her love for me was like that, almost like dying, like surrendering to death.

Was it the carefree nature of my youth, a poet's malady, or the influence of all the myths about death and resurrection that prevented me from being shocked when she talked about dying, unable to imagine that she—that high-spirited, vibrant young creature—was talking about the death of the body I so passionately loved, and instead made me think she meant it symbolically? He who wishes to create must die dozens of times in his life. He must separate, free himself from his nearest and dearest, from the soil, the country, family, friends, and especially from the ideas into which he has locked himself. No rebirth without first dying a certain death. Literature loves destruction in order to make new life possible. I wanted nothing more than to help her, like a midwife, to birth this poetic self. This child for us was the great unknown, as it is for all parents, and we had no idea that it would destroy everything and everyone, even itself.

Perhaps, at the time, I didn't yet realize all that. I understood it only after reading the journals, where I kept encountering the entanglement of rage and love, bobbing and weaving, the frivolous happiness she experienced when she risked everything, the need to feel death breathing down her neck to live. I read there how she used the ecstasy of the perilous ride, dangling from the stallion's neck, as a metaphor of yearning for her cruel lover in Paris, and how—eyes moist from the delight of having found an Adam—she merely changed the name of the character to make me the focus of the amorous image. I also saw her endlessly repeating the anecdote, as if searching for its meaning. What she experienced during the descent into the unknown and the ride on a bolting horse was the bliss of loss of control, of surrender to a real self, the only self with which she could love without hating herself for that love. She was imprisoned in the grip of a love colored by gratitude—the terrible trap of charity—and thought she could only truly love someone if she were unfettered, in free fall, liberated from the reins with which she was led by those who cared for her.

Less than four months after she made me hers by biting my cheek, we married in secret, without telling my family or our friends. It was a bare-bones ceremony in the church of Saint George the Martyr. It was raining, and as I pushed the ring onto her quivering finger, she wept. Standing there, brittle, pale, and trembling in a baby-pink dress, an expectant, tearful gaze turned upon me, glowing with bliss, she aroused in me a chivalry, tenderness, concern, and love I never knew I possessed, a dogged longing to protect her against all evil and guide her safely through the jungle.

I had never felt so wanted, so needed.

The overwhelming love she unleashed in me reminded me of the boy who'd brought home wounded birds from the woods and stuffed milk-soaked pieces of bread into their gaping little beaks until they had the strength to fly again.

James Joyce was the god who blessed our union. It was June 16, 1956, Bloomsday, and the day on which *Ulysses* begins and eventually ends with the litany of yeses: "Yes I will Yes." And I wanted it, yes, I wanted her, yes, as a woman, as a bride, as a child, yes, and everything I fearfully hid in a corner of my soul disguised itself as a humming faun who now and then hummed a tune: Bloomsday, doomsday.

The only family member present was her mother, who had come over from America to meet the man who was to become her son-in-law. Although they resembled each other and I could see the origins of my bride's pronounced cheekbones, characteristic nose, coal-dark eyes, and never-ending legs, from the first moment of our meeting, I wrestled with disgust at her mother's features, especially her mouth, and something in her gaze, a fleeting rigidity, piercing, severe, and frightening. She used that gaze to scrutinize me, the man who stood before the altar with her only daughter, in her eyes a country bumpkin of humble origins, dressed in black rags, without income or possessions, a poet of a few paltry verses, without name or fame.

I was initially impressed by the intelligence, erudition, and tense vigilance with which she kept an eye on everything in her immediate surroundings. But more than anything it was her effect on her firstborn—her crippled foal—that soon troubled me. In the early months of our acquaintance, I had sporadically seen that my love's spirits could change from one second to the next; she could transform from a jubilant creature into a fractious child, but in her mother's presence she shot like a flash of lightning back and forth between adoration and aversion, affection and irritation. She was more artificial and more authentic than I had ever seen before.

On the first night of Aurelia's stay in England, three days before our marriage, my bride had a nightmare from which I cautiously shook her awake. She was sobbing uncontrollably and said she despised herself for all the times the previous day when she'd behaved hatefully toward her mother. It was heartless, and she was overwhelmed with sympathy for the woman who had buried her own mother two months earlier, my bride's dear Viennese grandmother who had moved in with them after her father's death, the grandmother of the ocean and the stories, the music and the noodles, the grandmother who had heard her groaning in the cellar and to whom she owed her resurrection.

In daily life we try to make ourselves comprehensible by speaking the language of others in the hope that we will be understood, but at night, when rationality and social adaptation have shuffled off to sleep, an unbound self speaks to us in a language that is completely our own. I've always felt that my dreams were meaningful and worked at remembering them. To a poet, the subconscious is a repository of knowledge, artificially distorted by an ancient imagery with which he must become familiar—he must dare to decipher it because it contains a truth about himself that can only make itself known in a hermetic form. No one else dreams your dreams. The images—archaic and archetypical in their symbolism—are meant for you, delivered through that which is hidden and most essential in yourself. Anyone who has no access to that cryptic part of their personality remains a poet of greeting-card poetry, just as respectably and artistically fabricated as the persona with which we face the light of day and interact with others.

When it comes to the most important dream in my life, I don't remember whether it was a real dream or a daydream that crept in due to the weariness of the watchman. I was studying at Cambridge, English language and literature, under the misconception that this would be the ideal springboard for a poet. At my desk, bored, my reluctance growing, I labored over the weekly essay in which for the umpteenth time I would subject some writer's work to vivisection. Suddenly I felt there was someone or something in the room behind me. It approached slowly. When I turned my head, I saw a fox, or rather an emaciated man with a fox's head, charred black and bleeding, as if he had just escaped a fire. Rooted to the spot, I waited, tense but not fearful. The fox came closer, brought his head to eye level, and gave me a tormented look. The next thing I knew, he slammed down a man's bloodied hand onto the blank page in front of me. He bent toward me and whispered, "Stop . . . you are destroying us." He then disappeared as mysteriously as he had come. On the sheet of paper was a palm print in gleaming wet blood. The following day I informed the faculty of my decision to discontinue my studies in literature. I switched to social anthropology.

The night before we were married, I dreamt—as I so often do—that I was out fishing. I was sitting on the edge of the pond I knew from childhood, a rectangular pool between the hills, bordered by wispy trees. Fishermen are thinkers. Starting at the glistening water's surface, the line of the rod links you with a dark, invisible world. You hook into an ever-deepening, trancelike stillness toward your dark soul, your monsters. It was night. From the depths a pike rose and gave me a defiant look, flaunting its characteristic slow arrogance. Anyone who knows the pike—this merciless killer that eats its own species if necessary—knows that it is born with a menacing grin. No one escapes the intimidating power of its indelible disdain. We looked at one another, two predators, each in his own element, one in the air, the other in the water. I woke with the image of the staring pike and the blissful, fearful excitement of the fisherman who has just tested his strength against a monster, of the poet who has briefly stood eye-to-eye with everything he has been forced to conceal. And I knew that she was the one, my Pisces bride—with her poetic ascendant opposite my Neptune and eternally fixed in my tenth house, the house of revelation, of reputations good and bad—and that she gave me access to the deepest darkness, to the source of everything I dreamt of writing for the rest of my life. My sister—the serious diviner in our family—had reached a different interpretation of the portended marriage between our stars. In the conjunction of my bride's moon and my sun, she saw the harbinger of a hell of rivalry and jealousy, I that of a wild paradise. As for the Pisces in my house of fame, she had ominously remarked that this woman would change my name forever, would surround it with the stink of sulfur, but the double signs can be interpreted two ways, so to me, her explanation struck me as sisterly jealousy, and I interpreted the constellation as signifying the scent of glory.

We were young and inexperienced, hesitantly on our way to the world of adults, responsibilities, wages, houses, each in search of our own voice. We wrote every day, dreamt of a poetic life, had little money and a wealth of passion. Six days after our marriage, we travelled to the Continent for two months, she with a fully stuffed Samsonite in one hand, a portable Hermes in the other, I with a rucksack full of old clothes and a red-bound bible-paper Shakespeare under my arm. It was our first exercise in the nomadic existence for which—based on our youth, a certain talent for romantic pathos, and a shared admiration for Frieda and D. H. Lawrence—we seemed predestined. We fancied ourselves pilgrims in search of the highest significance that can be attributed to the word "we."

The evening before we left, we went to my local pub. We'd removed and hidden our wedding rings to conceal our newly married status, although we were both afraid the happiness was dripping from our faces and would betray our secret. Ignorant of the journey we were planning, one of my friends started up a ballad about newlyweds who discover on their honeymoon that they will sour one another's future lives. I sang along in full voice, incredulously anchored in my self-assured happiness.

We flew to Paris and took up residence at the aptly named Hôtel des Deux Continents. For two weeks we strolled along the streets while I remained in the dark about her anxiety over this glorious victory march, now that she was crisscrossing the city hand in hand with a bridegroom, at any moment in danger of coming eye-to-eye with the love who had betrayed her.

She kept quiet about the other man with whom she was walking.

I never told her that her Paris wasn't my Paris.

It seems only men live with the images and ghosts of past wars, of soldiers, leaders, and rebels, collaboration and resistance, murder, blood and mud, as if the feminine imagination stops at the threshold of our histories and resolutely refuses to enter the battlefields on which men—husbands, fathers, sons, brothers—sacrificed their lives and left behind millions of women, orphaned and widowed. I have yet to meet a woman who knows what the Maginot Line is, which battle was fought at Verdun, what the letters SS stand for, and why which war was fought where. Of course, as an American she did not know the war as I did, born and raised in a grieving valley, sodden with tears poured out for the men who'd disappeared, snatched away by the madness of the Great War, and again unmanned by World War II.

For her the last war was just a daily radio program, avidly listened to by her German forebears.

While she chattered on about cafés and terraces where Hemingway, Fitzgerald, and Stein had left prints on the glasses and cups with their transatlantic lips, about Picasso's genius, and the gift of the Impressionists' innovative gaze—we'll only ever see a sunrise through Monet's eyes—and poured all her Baedeker knowledge over me to silence her real Paris, the wailing Paris of her despair, I walked the quaysides of an occupied city, riddled with bullet holes, *collaborateurs*, and guerrilla fighters, draped with swastikas, surrounded by stomping Germans in uniform.

Poetry often comes into being despite ourselves, a truth that escapes us, that forces its way out between the selected concealments. It doesn't heed our desire to cover things up. I like silence, secrets, a wealth of meanings and associations that belong to me alone, but I had imagined myself as a transparent husband, a man who is known to his love as no other. The only thing was, like Cordelia, I didn't want to waste any words on it. Love, and be silent.

We travelled on to Spain, fulfilling one of my long-cherished wishes. Attracted by the primitive desolation of the country, in search of the drop of Moorish blood which my father claimed ran through our veins, I had been planning before we met to go and live in Spain for a year, paying my way by teaching English. Now, bound to a bride who had to finish her degree, I couldn't go a single day without her. We went together, for a month at least. We arrived in Madrid after an exhausting, sticky journey, each with our silent Paris in mind. On the train, I had noticed that she was less enthusiastic than me about the raw country, the unrelenting light, the desertlike dryness, and did her best not to complain about the dust, stench, thirst, dirt. In my gratitude for her brave stoicism, I was blind to the demons—shaken awake by a swaying train and her growing fear of everything she saw and heard yet couldn't comprehend—with which she wrestled in silence on the journey. So it didn't occur to me that the last thing she needed was to be taken to a bullfight.

On a Sunday afternoon we walked to the Plaza de Toros de Las Ventas del Espíritu Santo, a name which betrayed no hint of the cruel spectacle we were about to witness. We entered a gigantic, perfectly circular arena together with hundreds of other tourists and excited Spaniards, with her pressed close to me, anxious about what she was about to see—killing, death. I thought I would be unaffected by this primitive struggle, accustomed as I was to the battle between man and animal while hunting, animals torn open in traps, shooting and skinning game, the necessary slaughter of a suffering creature.

We sat front and center on a wooden bench, helplessly exposed to a burning sun, a bloodthirsty atmosphere, and billowing ocher sand. A fanfare of trumpets announced the parade of flamboyant picadors, muletas, and matadors, colorfully turned out in close-fitting costumes with gleaming gold stitching and tassels, the matador's left arm appearing deceptively powerless, covered in a sling, like cockerels and yet strangely feminine due to the tights, the pink stockings, and the ballet-like footwear. Everything was still peaceful medieval splendor when the first bull entered the arena, a shining blue-black animal, proudly horned with pointed weapons, looking around in surprise, innocent in the ignorance of his lot. In a flash his peace was disturbed when from all sides colorfully dressed men emerged to attract his attention with bright-orange capes, left and right. He didn't know where to look, sullenly stormed the nearest cape, gouged in vain at nothing when it was teasingly pulled away before his nose, and briefly stood still as if wondering how he had got into this absurd show. With the same bemusement, he stormed toward another cape, and another and another, swirling ever faster, turning elegantly, without noticing that he was exhausting himself in this futile chase and thus becoming easier prey for the death blow for which the dancers were skillfully preparing him. Sitting high upon a horse covered with jute mats, a picador dealt the sweaty bull his first wound from above, driving a spear into his broad neck.

On seeing the gushing blood—a crimson river on the black of the coat—my bride uttered a cry of horror, clutched my arm with both hands, and buried her face in my shoulder. "Don't, please," she said half crying. She was trembling like a sick bird, and that was when I realized we were in the wrong place, the wrong country even. It was not this bloody spectacle in broad daylight that she wanted to stop, but the cruel spectacle in her head, the nocturnal images of amputated legs, self-inflicted mutilations, stabbings, cuts, severed throats. She saw her own nightmares played out in the arena, under a spotlight that revealed everything.

I wanted to take her away as quickly as possible from the city associated with the rusty scent of blood and the scene of seven bulls' red corpses, dragged away through the dusty sand, the pink-white foam of a futile rage around their open mouths, the miserable finale of a proud existence, away from the matadors vomiting with fear, from the horses thrust high on the bulls' horns, from an audience inflamed by the proximity of death. We left early the next morning in search of a more peaceful Spain, of that part of a country most dear and familiar to her: the coast.

We travelled by bus via Alicante to Benidorm, still a small, old fishing village back then, where we found a cheap pension right beside the Mediterranean, in the home of a French-speaking widow who—like so many people once they find out you're a writer—beamingly claimed to be a writer too.

My bride was calmed, albeit briefly, by the nearness of the sea and her resolve to deal with the bullfight in a story. The interfering widow got on her nerves to such an extent that at night she couldn't sleep out of fear of being poisoned by the black-haired witch. After a week we fled to find accommodation some distance away. Since we were still discovering one another, it was only later that I saw the pattern, that it was never a man but always a woman who aroused her most primal fears. To her, a man was a source of desire—for love, for death—but death was always brought by a woman.

All her life she had been dependent on the benevolence of others, on her stifling mother's willingness to make sacrifices, on prizes and scholarships, on the psychological and financial support of a number of benefactresses, one of whom had become rich by writing a mediocre melodrama turned into a film script, while another had acquired regional fame by living her entire life as a feminist professor on the Smith campus with a female companion and a dog. All of these women saw in her an extension of themselves, the ideal projection of their aborted dreams, or a younger self in another time, when a writing woman would no longer be viewed with suspicion and scorn. Her fury—a healthy, rebellious rage—flared up when she had the idea that her life did not belong to her but was the property of her ambitious mother and these so-called wise women with life experience and dubious writing talent, who incessantly bombarded her with their moldy advice, and she was supposed to be grateful for this deceitful extortion to boot. When she said she felt like a whore, it was not because she had slept with several men, but because she felt she was the property of a condescending matriarchy, in a permanent state of indebtedness she had to redeem with a successful life. Sometimes—in yet another attempt to work out the mystery of her death—I think that her suicide was also the ultimate way to reclaim her own life. The angry child demanded it like a snatched plaything. In her despair and rage, she forgot that others were tied to that life. The children, me.

From the day I met her, she liberated me from everything that had hindered the flow of my writing, obstacles I couldn't even identify: stuffy England, cocky, class-conscious Cambridge, the desire for a muse—I don't know. She was a breath of fresh air blowing away the dusty lethargy of idleness, of having been promising for so long, someone whose friends expected him to become the greatest among them, without having many poems to justify the name. She read everything I wrote and had already written, cried and laughed about the phrases, celebrated their originality, gushed about their creator, and when she offered criticism, it was sharp-witted and fair, finding a weak point in the texture. Energetic and dedicated, she set herself the task of giving my name the fame she felt it deserved, stationing herself at the typewriter and typing everything out in triplicate with carbon copies, placing them in envelopes, and sending them like gospels into the world, convinced with a heavenly trust that my word must be revealed.

I see her before me in every room we inhabited—in London, Cambridge, Paris, Benidorm, Boston, Devon—how in the meager lamplight, her long back upright, she typed out our work at the piano of language, her fluttering fingers dancing across the keys, unimaginably quick, the typing like rain on a thatched roof, the carriage return like a machine gun. And I remember a happiness that seemed too big for my body. Just before we began our honeymoon, the first acceptances from literary magazines came in, adorned with American stamps, and she greedily tore them open and leapt upon me shrieking with joy.

There are many ways in which writers succeed in hiding their true selves. Although her genius tried to break through and in some sentences triumphed, I always detested the pretentious formalism of her early work, however competent and skillful. It was the nectar, the enticing perfume, the deceptive lure of a false self. Of course you can write about dichotomies, caryatids, and epitaphs if the same couplet throws in some rabbit droppings, lipstick, and a tear-drenched tissue. The poems, the prose, every word that she laboriously pressed from the rigid pen, were tailored to the market, intended to conquer a place in the pantheon of the *New Yorker* or to be sold as a popular commodity to prissy women's magazines, adapted to the expectations of the readership, risking nothing, predictable and commercial. It was the reason my friend Daniel—before he got to know her—stamped her poetry as "fraud," an accusation of which she regularly reminded me and which she said thundered through her head like a steamroller. The better I got to know her, the better I understood that in a single word Daniel had touched on her latent fear of exposure.

She had no imagination. She had paid with a personal experience for every image, symbol, and carefully unearthed metaphor—always aided by the indispensable *Roget's Thesaurus*. Since she was not free, the pen riveted to her, hopelessly indebted to a reality she had experienced but lacking the courage to be honest, she was always afraid that her poetic reservoir would run dry. One day she would look back on a plotless oeuvre held together by nothing other than a dead father, a suicide attempt, and the imbalance between love and work.

It was a genuine fear. Writers so closely connected to autobiography narrow their work to an individual fate, missing the universal and the sacred, the world where everything is connected from the beginning of time. They also miss literature, in which our forebears narratively shaped what it means for humans to live.

Everything about my bride moved me, but this inability to be herself, the panicked quest for an honest voice, touched me the most. She was cut off from the purest part of herself, where her creativity and genius resided, bound to her wounds, wrath, and ruthlessness. That sense of being cut off was the source of her frustration and despair. The well-behaved, ambitious girl's rationalizations held her back from what was ambiguous, complex, obscure, and violent, from her true nature. And I believed that the highest act of love was to liberate her like a knight of the Round Table from the dungeon of a dark interior, to lead her out and pass her the holy grail of free imagination.

Before long, she trusted me enough so that I could slowly begin making cracks in her armor of deceptive cheerfulness. She was as sensitive to my voice as a newborn lamb to the bleating of the mother sheep, so, after two failed attempts, I managed to hypnotize her completely. I could control her digestion, blood circulation, breathing, and finally her dreams with my voice. When it became clear how receptive she was—I was even able to influence the duration of her menstrual periods and in part eliminate their pain—I went deeper.

Hypnosis is intimate. We were together: one spirit, one body. She lay motionless on the bed, hands folded on her stomach, a harbinger of the complete defenselessness of a dead body turned to brittle stone, surrendered to the gaze of the survivors.

"Close your eyes."

I talked and looked at that young, beautiful face, bent over her, my voice close to her ear, to the scar under her eye. Step by step I accompanied her to the edge of the river, had her carefully take a seat in the rocking boat and travel like Charon over the Styx. My voice followed the meter of the oar strokes, deeper and deeper into the crypts of the subconscious, every stroke carrying her further from that mannerist self, from rationality, from deception. She heard the water sweetly lapping against the prow, relaxed, her breathing slowed, her limbs went limp. We travelled to the other side, to the bank where she had to let go of the final handhold in order to brave the step toward the unknown and unpredictable, toward the wounded child, the furious woman, the writer.

No matter how many times we tried, she never stepped out of the boat on the other side. Once moored, she shied away from dropping the safe armor of pretense, from the death of the all-controlling self. As soon as her hands started to move, I knew I had lost her, that she was pushing her way out of the embrace of my voice. Slowly she unclasped her hands—I could do nothing other than watch the dissolution of our bond. I spoke on, using the same timbre, perhaps a little more insistently, to keep her with me. But the same thing always happened. The liberated left hand buckled and hooked like a claw into my hair, lip, jaw. She stared at me, eyes wide open, still half in an underground world, a mix of fear and trust in her gaze.

"You have too much power over me," she said. "I don't want to die."

We had planned to remain in Spain until the end of September, but—however thrifty our lifestyle—by the end of August we had to use the last of our money to return home. During the trip, which took days, via Barcelona and Paris, I pondered our honeymoon, the idyllic days and nights, the intimacy of working together in a small room, the daily stream of stories I had easily set down on paper, simple fables with a profound undertone, and how I read them to her while she cooked on the single-ring gas hob, ingenious recipes fished out of the cookbook she had brought, the room fragrant with garlic, onions, and tomatoes. Swimming in the sea, sunbathing, the daily walk to the market and how she sketched the tradesmen there, sitting sidesaddle, the tip of her tongue between her teeth, a girl in white socks, beautiful in her concentration and peace. But I also remembered the ballad I'd belted out with the others before our departure and everything that had moved and troubled me over those weeks. Our first crushing fight about God knows what, how enraged and remote she suddenly was, how inaccessible I felt myself, two powerless strangers next to one another, imprisoned in their own correctness, the air around us poisoned by a sulking silence, and then the fear that things might stay that way, the dream of an ideal marriage already in tatters, broken beyond repair. And the morning that she woke up feeling sick and feverish—from a bug or a bad oyster—her growing fear of dying in a backward country, without pills, doctors, hospitals, the incessant crying and moaning, and I made a hearty soup, which I fed to her spoon by spoon, and I recoiled, thinking that it was much ado about a mere 101-degree fever, doubting the seriousness of the illness, for the first time finding her hysterical.

We had good reason to keep quiet about our marriage and to justify the resulting lies—as a married woman she would lose her scholarship— but bearing false witness before my friends and in letters to my family weighed heavily upon me. This was not the behavior they had come to expect of me. I felt bad for my mother, who—after her eldest son had emigrated to Australia and married there—had now missed a second wedding. After our return to England, completely penniless, we travelled on to Yorkshire to stay a few weeks with my parents at the Beacon in Heptonstall. On the train, I felt like a schoolboy going to confess a misdemeanor to his parents, but when I looked at the young woman opposite me—glowing with health and zest for life, silently immersed in Emily Brontë—my love for her justified every sin.

An early autumn adorned the hilly landscape with the subdued colors of decay, a death dressed up in rusty brown and bright red to add luster to its transience and promise a grandiose comeback. I knew every inch of the land I was ushering her into—the scent of the valley, the heaths and meadows, how the wind howled between the dry stone walls, where the mushrooms shot out of the ground, the beeches in which the squirrels danced, where clear water flowed from springs, deer rose from the mist— and I looked forward to seeing the familiar landscape through her eyes.

In Cambridge, I could not have imagined a more appreciative audience than my child of the ocean. On the long walks we took there—where, like a jaunty guide, I named plants and flowers, recognized birds by their song or flight, fed her nuts and berries—she accompanied me in wonder, embraced me every ten paces, and her happiness made me proud and rich in a way I had never felt before, a duplicated man from whose body a woman had been taken who belonged inseparably with him and would never again disappear from his life. When we came across an owl half hidden behind the leaves of a copse, I performed the most splendid masterpiece, sucking a rabbit's cry of fear from my closed fist, the imitation so true to life that the bird of prey flew at my face, wings splayed. But a couple of days later, she outdid me by climbing onto a rickety fence and declaiming Chaucer to twenty surprised cows. For several minutes the large-eyed audience stood rooted to the spot in the swampy earth, incapable of freeing themselves from a melodious voice addressing them in faultless Middle English as the Wyf of Bathe.

Every day we walked in the countryside, and sometimes on longer walks we lay on my outspread coat two or three times while I made love to her under the naked firmament, with the sun and a few nervous rabbits as witnesses to our wild passion. Our bodies crushed the ants, wood lice, and centipedes, insects whose Latin names she served up effortlessly—*Formica rufa, Armadillidium vulgare, Scutigera coleoptrata*—linguistic acrobatics with which she delighted me and which she had already perfectly mastered by the time she was five for the sake of Daddy. The Prussian professor of entomology, with his proud fondness for drilling ideas into his pupils, had pounded Linnaeus's nomenclature into her young head.

I am attached to the landscape of my youth and to my family. My brother's emigration to the other side of the world knocked a hole in me that I spent the rest of my life trying to close by dreaming of a reunion with the man dearer to me than all others. Before I met my bride—and found in her a brother—I had planned to follow him, to move to Australia, near him, imagining that I would find that lost paradise there, that we would be reunited and go on endless hikes and hunting trips, sit on a riverbank, talking or silent, in a way that was impossible with anyone else. My years with her, the seven years of our marriage, were the only years of my life in which the pain of that longing was dampened. No other woman after that was able to still my yearning to be with Gerald.

In the train on the way north she recollected the caustic jealousy she'd felt when her brother, Warren, was born—she'd been two and a half years old, queen of a lonely realm—and she asked whether I had been jealous of the oldest son, my predecessor.

"No," I said, "I don't believe so."

Having grown up in a grieving valley, familiar with the phenomenon that the women's greatest love was not destined for the men around them but for those who had disappeared, snatched away by the war, I understood my mother's grief, and at night when I heard smothered sobs from my parents' bedroom, I cried along inaudibly. I watched my bride as I told the story and saw her eyes slowly fill with tears until they overflowed and two shining rivulets trailed over her brown cheeks.

My parents were waiting for us in the doorway of the Beacon in their Sunday best. I was so touched that I had to swallow a lump in my throat when I introduced my American bride. I saw a brief flash of hurt in my mother's eyes, but she recovered her composure when I explained why we had had to keep our marriage secret and added that we would still celebrate the real wedding all together, someday, somewhere. As soon as my bride stepped over the threshold, it was as if the interior changed, the dark colors brightened, and even my father and mother became lighter, almost frivolous. Her natural impertinence—restrained by an equally natural timidity—loosened my parents' tongues; I saw them relax with the calm of country folk, to satisfy her hunger for knowledge. The stories and rumors I'd so often heard suddenly gained a significance I'd not previously attributed to them, thanks to the rapture with which she listened and replayed them to me at night in bed—enthusiastically distorted, interpreted, and colored from an American perspective, gaining the weight of poetry, of literature.

She had finished *Wuthering Heights* and immediately started again from the beginning, completely under the spell of the all-consuming love between Cathy and Heathcliff, and she said we were they, Cathy and Heathcliff, and that they were one person. "'I am Heathcliff.'" She quoted her romantic heroine with glittering eyes, and I confirmed it with a smile, and said, "Yes, you're Heathcliff, I'm Heathcliff."

Wearing sturdy shoes, with the novel as a literary atlas in her red handbag, she'd been waiting impatiently for an hour for my uncle Walter, who—impressed by my exotic sweetheart—had offered to be our guide to the desolate heights. I walked behind them, ready to catch her if she slipped on the mossy stones. She listened to my uncle's animated stories while he behaved as if he had known the Brontë sisters personally and had visited them on a daily basis. In his view, they were a couple of withered wretches, never experienced anything, all of it made up, the three of them at the top of the hill, sitting around a table fabricating stories, wasting away with tuberculosis, afraid of real life, afraid of love, afraid of ghosts and of God. She kept turning to me, beaming broadly, the heath wind reddening her cheeks, arms outstretched to encompass the elusive landscape, my Cathy, my Emily. That day, the ominous clouds, the purple heather, the fields, sheep, trees, and ruins did their utmost, like a fully equipped theater company, to offer the most colorful backdrop they could muster for the romantic drama. Out of pure joy at their generosity, I applauded my country and its writers, startling a couple of dozing crows, who—flapping black against a gray background—proved themselves entirely capable of perfecting the pastoral image.

Hidden from my uncle, anxiously clinging to me, she burst into tears behind a maple tree. I thought it was fatigue from the hours of walking, climbing the steep hills, the overwhelming impression of a novel come true, but no, she sobbed, it was none of those things, it was the transience, the remains of a life, of Emily's life, motherless, dead at the age of thirty, a single novel to her name, published a year before her death, under a pen name—that too—and that as a writer she had never known how famous she would become, a worldwide, posthumous fame which had led a reader on this day, all the way from Massachusetts, to the Wuthering Heights to look for her, Emily Brontë, and that—she was ashamed of it—the monster of jealousy had suddenly bitten her in the calf. She was so childishly sad, and I thought it so funny, that I struggled not to laugh.

I've often thought back to that trip to the desolate heights, the tears behind the maple tree, the way she was torn between compassion and envy, and how Emily Brontë's lot so closely mirrored her own future that I have thought—occasionally—that she copied it. I sang "Waltzing Matilda" for her on the way back, and she—desperately cheerful again—sang along with the now-familiar song, slightly off-key. She stopped me shortly before we reached my parents' house and said, "You watch out, when I'm dead, I'll come and haunt you, like Cathy, like the swagman from 'Waltzing Matilda.'"

"Then I'll dance with you," I said.

Lectures started in early October, and I took her by bus to Leeds. I was to stay another month with my parents, then—under the pressure of our secret marriage—teach English in Madrid for the three-quarters of a year she needed to finish her degree. Once all that was behind us, we could leave for America in the late spring. On the platform she choked back her tears and I promised to come to Cambridge as soon as possible, but when the train pulled away, with her blowing kisses at me from behind the window until she disappeared from sight, I was left with the same acute sense of abandonment I had felt when I waved my brother off for his military service in the RAF. On the way back to Heptonstall, that loss was accompanied by a black melancholy. Nothing had happened during those weeks to explain this sorrow. The way she competed with my mother, seeking to win over my taste buds with less stodgy fare than stews and pies, merely amused me, and I had proudly concluded that my mother simply had no talent for being challenged by any other woman whatsoever. Later, much later, after I'd read my bride's transatlantic letters—those dreadful documents of false jubilation, exaggeration, and fanaticism—I asked Aurelia to omit a sneering remark about my mother's cooking. She had been dead for years, but the comment hurt me as if she were reading over my shoulder and had been posthumously stabbed in the back by my bride.

To spare my parents my inward mood, I walked past our house to the church and the graveyard, wandered among the headstones, read the familiar surnames of local people. Without knowing it, I was standing on the ground where, seven years later, I would bury my wife and add an outsider's name like a foreign body to the English alphabet of the dead. I was overcome with an incomprehensibly profound grief, mixed with fear and dread of the future.

What had seemed on the morning of her departure like gloom and grief turned out to be the first seeds of a festering restlessness which increased the longer we were apart. I slept badly, could barely concentrate, was never hungry, wandered about like a man whose body had been half amputated. The days without her were wasted time, and I knew she was pining away in her room in college in exactly the same way. The only benefit of the separation was that we could now write to one another. Every morning at eight o'clock, I stood at the gate waiting for the postman to come cycling along the bumpy road, and every day with a knowing grin, he handed me a letter from Cambridge. In the bedroom—lying on the bed in which I still saw the impression of her body, still smelled her scent—I read the sighing, ironic sentences, heard her voice in every word, saw a pair of dark-brown eyes shining with excitement, and the restless pain made way for the burning longing for the game of sun and moon. The hours I spent with the extensive epistles, drawings, and poems, and sat at my table writing her similarly expansive letters, were the only time in which I didn't feel split, hacked apart like a lump of wood. What we could talk about for hours, we now wrote: the books we were reading, the poems we were working on, who we had run into and what they had to say. I continued picking at the tight bands of the corset in which she had tied herself so that she could write more than four sentences without running out of breath.

Thinking is a discipline that takes time, a holy time which—like the monastic Matins, Lauds, and Vespers—must be consciously set aside to protect it from the intrusive power of the banal. Thinking itself is something I like to think about, because for the writer it is both friend and foe, necessity and obstacle. I was—am—convinced that thinking can be taught, and like an acolyte I assisted my bride—in answer to her worrying that she didn't know how she should think about a story, novel, or poem—teaching her to pray, to enter a half trance in which forced, abstract thought makes way for poetic, creative thought, for which you have to descend into yourself, into your secret memories, preserved because the event contains a concealed truth intent on revealing itself, even if it goes against the grain. The deeper you go, the closer you come to what is sacred, universally human, freed from the limited biographical consciousness. Besides being a rational creature, man is an animal, equipped with a purely intuitive intelligence, the egocentric seed in search of an egg, of the perfect other in which it can sacrifice itself by melting into it so that something new can be born, the essence of every creation. Exploring your inner life without recognizing your animal origin and heritage is empty, false, abstract. You have to dare to jump, to let go of your handhold, to arrive at a real self. You recognize the originality of a writer in the courage with which he has dared to leap into the abyss. And in the depth of that abyss.

Our neighbors in London weren't best pleased with my habit, when reading a poem out loud, of accompanying myself on an African drum—or on a pan or bucket—on which I beat out the rhythm of the phrases, or pacing up and down, stamping out the measure of a quatrain and showing her with a Charlie Chaplinesque stumble what happens when a poem doesn't scan. I don't remember if she had already confessed to being tone deaf. At home, in my bedroom, I continued in epistolary obedience to my vocation as a teacher and liberator, advised her to read all poems out loud, learn at least one a day by heart, supplied her with plots for stories, commented on new verse, recommended Blake as an antidote to that asinine Augustine—someone who at least understands that good and evil are inextricably bound—and in every letter, I let her know how terribly I missed and desired her—my ponk my puss my darling my divine wife. Nothing could make up for my yearning for her physical proximity, not even the acceptances streaming in from magazines willing to publish our poems—the first glimmer of a long-awaited success.

It was impossible.

The imminent prospect of spending seven or eight months in Spain without her became increasingly oppressive to me, and the tone of her letters became alarmingly somber. The BBC's offer to record me reading Yeats's poems for a series of radio broadcasts came at an opportune moment, and I fell over myself in my haste to pack my rucksack and leave for London. I hadn't seen her for thirteen days. It felt like an eternity.

Early on Friday morning I stepped out of the train at King's Cross, where we had arranged to meet. I saw her storming toward me against the current of disembarking passengers. She shouted my name, shrieked, uttered cries of relief as she ran, her long arms windmilling in the air, and leapt at me like a boisterous dog, crying uncontrollably as if I had risen from the dead, a miracle. She was beside herself and attempted, floundering breathlessly, to explain the magnitude of this biblical joy. She had wanted to surprise me, had taken an earlier train from Cambridge, got off at the bus terminal where she thought she could catch me before I took the train to King's Cross, sat there for hours—two—waiting for the bus, for me, her bridegroom, and then everyone got off but me. Total panic—where was I? She jumped onto the bus, stopped short of looking under the seats, described me in detail to the driver—he's gigantic, almost six foot, sickeningly good-looking, smooth dark hair, a little greasy perhaps, a thick curl over his forehead, to the right, so cute, and he keeps casually sweeping it back with a beautiful, broad hand, smiling vaguely about nothing, or at least you don't know why, there's always something going on in his head, you can see that, and it may be that he looks like a scruffy tramp, but he's not, he's a great poet, a genius, he'll be world-famous someday, surely the driver noticed that passenger, such charisma, such an aura, truly he had transported a god in his bus, had he really not seen him? And then she jumped into a taxi, dashed through London's rush hour to King's Cross, her heart in her mouth, urging the driver on because it was a matter of life and death, and once there she rushed onto the platform full of anxious suspicions and behold, there I was, alive and well, not wiped off the face of the earth, and because my train had been delayed—a twist of fate—we arrived on the platform at exactly the same time; it was an omen, the gods were watching over us and we were meant for one another, for all eternity.

I looked into that tearful face and, grinning, experienced the sensation of being an outright miracle.

We'd made plans for the weekend—seeing friends, a visit to the Tate, strolling along the Thames, or visiting the zoo—but we did nothing, we stayed in. I went to my meeting with the BBC, we did the shopping, but the world was an oversized coat and as soon as we could, we returned to my friend Daniel's apartment, locked the door, cooked together, ate and drank, crawled into bed, or remained sitting at the table, happy to be together in one room, close to each other. In the morning I told her what I had dreamt and how I interpreted the images. She said she was envious of the poetic wealth of that language, its composition and structure, and that the pitiful, fragmentary repetition of ghostly images with which she was saddled at night made her miserable. I came up with some exercises to carry her with me into my dreams and explained how, before she fell asleep, she could set the mind tasks for its nocturnal work. On the third morning she told me about a dream which was similar to mine. I didn't know she had made it up to be close to me, but those three days did make me realize that we were both sick, miserable, and unhappy about being apart. Something had to change.

On the day that she went to confess our concealed marriage, I imagined how she knocked on her supervisor's door at Cambridge—nervous, resolute, and, I hoped, not too heavily armed with the irrational rage which overcame her when she felt backed into a corner. As a married student she ran the risk of being sent down, but divulging the secret was the only way we could live together.

Her supervisor warmly congratulated her.

Less than a month later we found our first apartment in Cambridge, on the ground floor of 55 Eltisley Avenue, small, filthy, dilapidated, but dirt cheap and close to the fields and woods where we so often made early-morning excursions to see the sunrise.

I was as relieved and happy as she, but it ate away at me that all those lies—misleading friends and family, twisting and turning, the panic—had been unnecessary, caused by a chimera. I had allowed myself to be swept along by her specters of punishment, condemnation, and excommunication, and she—however temporarily—had possessed the power to make me someone I was not and never wanted to be, a liar, a coward, rather than a man who stands up for himself regardless of the cost.

My parents' sympathy toward her did me good. Now that I had grown used to the aversion she sometimes aroused, it became clear that the warm welcome they gave her was much less tiresome than having to ignore my friends' critical glances when we met in a pub or someone's room and my bride drew attention to herself in a way they considered affected, extravagant, or theatrical. Although I hoped I was wrong, my gut instinct was that my sister Olwyn, two years my senior, would not share my parents' enthusiasm. I looked forward to seeing her again after a long absence and to introducing the two women, but I suspected there was scant reason for optimism. It was no accident that we had twice missed her in Paris, where she lived. Coincidence is often more prudent than our own will.

She spent three days scrubbing, polishing, reorganizing, and repairing— a lick of paint here, a rug there—to make our first home as inviting as possible. She went over and over the menu with me, opted for roast beef, roast lamb, rabbit stew, roast beef after all, had me pick between ten different potato recipes, seven types of vegetable, asked endlessly whether Olwyn liked this or preferred that—questions to which I generally didn't know the answers—and on the morning she arrived was exhausted and at the end of her tether.

I saw it immediately. The first signs of displeasure and antipathy broke through the civilized goodwill the moment they said hello.

My bride was adept at keeping up appearances for long periods, but my sister was terrible at hiding her resentment. They shook hands. Olwyn—who clearly even in Paris had been unable to shake off our Celtic bluntness—sized up her brand-new sister-in-law a little too conspicuously, raised an eyebrow, and only then granted her an obliging smile. That circumflex accent was not lost on my bride. Sensitive even to a subcutaneous muscle contraction in the face of someone to whose judgment she was exposed, she was so grateful for Olwyn's approval that she gave her a boisterous American-style hug, a gesture that made my sister cringe. Things went from bad to worse when—on the assumption that a bond between women is most easily formed by deviously criticizing other women—after dinner, enthusiastic, spirited, and somewhat disinhibited, she painted one merciless portrait after another of her bigoted female teachers and stiff fellow students. She forgot that she was talking about English women and that my chain-smoking, cosmopolitan sister was English to the bone. It also didn't help that my bride spent the entire evening with her legs drawn up on the sofa, snuggled up against me like a cat, and planted at least forty kisses on my neck. When I dropped Olwyn off two days later to catch the train to Paris, she said nothing, but everything in her countenance said that marrying this woman was the biggest mistake of my life.

In order to earn money to live on and for the voyage to America, planned for the coming spring, I reluctantly took a job that winter at a boys' secondary school, teaching working-class children who were just past that receptive age when they can still learn to think independently and who were being obediently and willingly primed for the same miserable life as their uneducated, toiling parents. The hours I spent in front of the class rather than writing and reading were a high price to pay. I told myself that this was the life of a grown man with responsibilities, suppressed my feelings of loss, and cycled back to 55 Eltisley in the dark. My bride cycled back and forth to the university each day and awaited me in the evenings in a spotless house that smelled of dinner. As soon as I closed the door, the fatigue and melancholy fell away, I forgot the boys and my vain efforts to open the way to another life for them, and tried to make every hour with her last an eternity. The cold and damp of the earth rose through the foundations. Thickly wrapped in woolen jumpers and shawls, we talked, wrote, drew, and read, huddled near to the hearth, feet on a chair or table, or opposite one another on the sofa, legs intertwined.

On October 27, 1956—the first of her birthdays that I celebrated with her, the day she turned twenty-four, an age that now moves me, so young—I gave her a pack of tarot cards, explained the symbolism of the images—the path to wisdom, the difference between the major and minor arcana—and a book explaining the history of the game and its connections with Isis, Thoth, and Cabala. She was enthusiastic and—ambitious in everything—wanted to know more. Since we were always inventing ways of escaping an ordinary teacher's daily grind, she envisaged us, like the Yeatses, receiving people at home to draw their charts and read their cards for a fee. We chuckled at the prospect, didn't take ourselves seriously, but we talked about it often enough and never completely dismissed the plan.

Astrology, tarot, Ouija boards, hypnosis, Jung and the collective subconscious, Cabala—all the esoteric knowledge I'm fascinated with has a bad reputation, and all my life I have endlessly had to defend my interest in it against other people's skepticism. They thought they could attack me with rational arguments, talked about scientific proof, verifying predictions, about belief and superstition. But it's not a question of whether I believe something.

It's about language, metaphors.

It's about the primeval structure of stories and characters.

What annoys me about conventional psychology and sociology is the disregard for wisdom set down since ancient times in myths, folktales, fables, and in the poetic, prescientific manner in which it is represented. There is no such thing as "new man." He will always have a body and a mind, and his psyche is as restricted in its equipment as the body with its head, trunk, arms, legs, water, blood, and innards. What looks like a modern insight into man and the world is the same old story that's been around for thousands of years, played by the same characters, except it's repeatedly cast in a different form. Anyone who knows the myths sees them recur in infinite guises: heroes and cowards, masters and servants, gods and fallen angels; betrayal, cruel death, and resurrection; fragmentation and restoration of unity; the doppelgänger; the mischief and machinations of cheats and tricksters; condemnation, punishment, and redemption of the sinner; forbidden love between a man and woman of enemy tribes; the woman as virgin, mother, and hag; the quest for ultimate knowledge, for the real self; rebellion against the father, against the law, against one's own nature. This is seen, interpreted, and described in a more expressive, richer language than that of science. In order to make predictions, you only have to follow the thread of a known destiny, the inevitable plot of an ancient story, the tragedy of the archetype. If you encounter an Icarus, you know that someday he has to fall. If you sleep next to Dr. Jekyll, you know you might wake up beside Mr. Hyde. And if you meet an Electra, you know she will murder her mother, or the mother in herself.

We rigged up the Ouija board ourselves, cut the letters of the alphabet out of magazines and newspapers, laid them out in a circle on the coffee table, with a "Yes" and a "No" at the ends, and placed a glass in the middle. In Cambridge and London my friends and I had spent evenings huddled in a circle, our index fingers on a glass, often roaring with laughter about the messages we received, and my bride wanted to be initiated into this ritual. Cutting out the letters had reminded her of her time in the lunatic asylum, when, after her resurrection, language disappeared, and she could no longer read and write. At Smith College she had found a father figure in her literature lecturer and had asked for him in hospital. Dr. Beuscher had forbidden more or less every visitor—especially her mother—but Mr. Crockett was allowed in. For five months he visited his student every week to help her—through childish games and the patience of an angel—reclaim the erased alphabet letter by letter from oblivion. As usual she told the story as a quip, painting herself as a drooling child, bloated from the insulin treatment, but tears prickled in my eyes at the image of the devoted teacher on the edge of her bed. She saw it, embraced me, and asked sadly why she was like that, why she always had to be derogatory about people she had loved so dearly.

"You're afraid of abandonment," I said.

She was tireless, my bride, bursting with energy. As soon as she had arrived home, prepared for lectures the next day, cooked, baked, scrubbed, and washed, she would sit down at the typewriter to type out our work, add a cover letter, and send it out into the world. Since our reunion, I'd barely been able to keep up with the stream of poetic ideas and inspirations. I'd written every day, one poem after another. She kept a meticulous journal, in hot pursuit of a life that wasn't lived until it was described, sent letters to her mother weekly and to her brother occasionally, worked laboriously at a novel, and now and then wrote a poem. Besides Shakespeare and Yeats, we liked to read our own poems out loud to one another, offered comments where needed, polished them, read them out again.

In the first winter of our marriage—besides countless rejections, which to her were like a red rag to a bull, unleashing an even more furious creative drive—we received some initial praise, the first acceptances from renowned magazines, requests for more material, and a modest extra income.

By the time we sat down at the Ouija board, it was usually late and, exhausted from our concentrated efforts, we rested our fingertips on the glass, summoning spirits to take over the arduous brainwork, to inspire, thrill, or entertain us.

Waiting for movement is like fishing, at once exciting and relaxing. Will something happen? Is there anything beneath the surface? Is there some life I can't yet see, making itself known only when it takes the bait? What will come to light?

The first time I sat with my bride at the board, pen and paper at hand, we sent an invitation into the ether or to our subconscious minds—Is anybody there?—and waited. Suddenly, the upturned glass nosed over to "Yes." She gave me a mistrustful look—she wasn't buying it. She suspected that in my impatience, I'd pushed it toward the left corner. I denied it. If we do anything, we do it together. That's the magic of our intermingling. I showed her how little pressure I'd put on the glass, my finger resting on it as lightly as hers. To put her in charge and give her some practice, I said she should ask who we were dealing with. The glass crisscrossed the alphabet, muddled, incoherent, without revealing a legible name. When we asked if it was a man, it shot toward the right corner. Apparently not. Flushed with excitement, she asked about her father, her grandmother, our future. Whomever we'd managed to hook—either from the other side or from somewhere within us—the answers were obscene, gloomy, sinister. It seemed like some foulmouthed shrew or other was taking pleasure in snarling at my bride, barking out short answers—*Vixen, slut*—saying that the godforsaken dead were rotting in their graves and nothing was left except some dried old bones, and it wouldn't be long—*Scrawny whore*—before the maggots would be gnawing away at her cursed future.

It was a few weeks before we shook off that brutal initiation, but eventually we were able to laugh about it, make fun of the pathetic visitor, and she was ready for another go. The second time was better, and the times after that as well. We conducted lively discussions with various spirits, picked up new ideas for our work, and now and then jotted down a handsome phrase or a poem in the rough.

I'm not sure exactly when a spirit calling himself Pan first materialized, but he became a regular visitor—jocular, always mocking, crude, and never completely trustworthy. Our household god turned out to be both a joker and an avid gambler who promised to make our fortune in the weeks to come by accurately predicting the football pools. I wrote down his surprising prediction of thirteen draws, bought a pools coupon, filled it in—dreaming of the seventy-five thousand pounds in the pot. I was astonished when he appeared to have been mostly right, adrift by just one game.

It happened one evening when the air had lost its chill, and during the day we could make out the first signs of approaching spring in the young green blades pushing their way curiously up through the carpet of wet leaves. With so many changes on the horizon—an end to a cold winter, her graduation, and our departure for America—and given our increasingly amicable relationship with Pan, I plucked up the courage to ask our ill-mannered oracle the question I assumed—no, knew—obsessed my bride. I bent over the board and asked if we would become famous. The impact was catastrophic and defied all my expectations. With audacious strength Pan showed us why panic was named after him: he gave us the fright of our lives, as if we had become overly familiar and not been sufficiently respectful of his divinity. Out of nowhere an angry puppeteer abruptly pulled up my bride's hand, her eyes shot full of frightened tears, and—having wanted only to please her, chasing after the American dream of a glorious existence like an obedient old sheepdog—I listened, stunned, as she spoke in tongues. Pan dispensed with the slowness of the alphabet and spoke directly through her in a deep, eerie growl, mocking her longing for that hollow display, and asked whether she realized that the fame she so passionately desired would destroy everything she had.

In November I selected forty poems, titled the collection *The Hawk in the Rain*, and dedicated it to my wife. We walked to the letter box and, with stately solemnity, slipped the large envelope, which contained the requisite sixty pages, through the slot. To make the precious dispatch more personal, instead of addressing it to the Poetry Center in New York, she had written the names of the jury members in full—Mrs. Moore, Mr. Spender, and Mr. Auden—hoping the gesture would make an impression. She'd had a vision in which she'd seen me winning the debut prize for poetry with this collection, saw the book becoming a bestseller in England and America, kicking off the victory lap toward the pantheon.

I wasn't convinced.

Because my heart was divided, I hid my aversion to the word "bestseller" along with my shame at putting the most holy thing I possessed onto the block for something as vulgar as a competition, allowing myself to be meekly dragged along on the hunt for success, while at the same time understanding that following the path her tenacity had cleared for me was the only way to ensure being read. I cherished the image of the poet as my soul's property, anchored deep within me, independent of whatever glory the outside world could bestow. I had to resist the feeling that her mercantile spirit was corrupting the purity of my love for poetry. One of the least attractive legacies of my origins is that I've always been overly obsessed with money, ever on the hunt for ways of supporting myself as a poet. But earning money with poetry bordered on the verboten.

On February 23, 1957, two days before the anniversary of our first meeting, a telegram arrived at 55 Eltisley. The New York Poetry Center congratulated me on winning their First Publication Award. My ambivalence evaporated. We sang and danced exuberantly through the room, she cheering, "I knew it, I knew it," and I thanked her and kissed her. She rushed to phone her mother, even though it was the middle of the night on the other side of the Atlantic.

When I left for Cambridge, my English teacher, Mr. Fisher—there's really no such thing as coincidence—had given me a book that's still in my possession, along with the collected Blake and Shakespeare. The book, Robert Graves's *The White Goddess*, is well thumbed and has been read over and over again. It was the early 1950s, and I remember my shock at reading it, as if I'd been rudely robbed of the secret world I'd inhabited since the age of thirteen. I'd cherished until then the infantile fantasy that she showed herself only to me and that, thanks to reading all the myths and folktales, my view of her wonders and cruelty was completely unique. But everything I believed I had figured out for myself had already been thought of for me. Once I humbly digested that difficult lesson, I was finally able to accept Graves's mastery, and his work became the guiding light for the next phase of my life, one in which I no longer wallowed in the romanticism of uniqueness, but dedicated my life to the highest goal: serving poetry and striving for sacred unification with all living things.

I was twenty-one and wandering restlessly with one of Graves's most important lessons: that a poet can become fully aware of his poetic self only once he falls in love with a woman in whom the white goddess resides, someone who unites creation and destruction and who will bring triumph and doom into his life. Graves's concept of love and hate, *odi atque amo*, became an intriguing formula accompanying me on my quest because I had not yet experienced a love that was also capable of arousing my hatred.

Five years later I had become the poet I'd longed to be, awards and all, besotted and tripping the light fantastic with my capricious muse, profoundly convinced that she was the white goddess with a thousand names.

Married, crammed together in a tiny apartment, hemmed in by an icy English winter, I soon discovered that one of her names was Hera. She spun the most incredible fairy tales about the hours I spent out of her sight, imagined clandestine affairs with other women, or was afraid I was daydreaming about girlfriends past and future. While I was declaiming "The Waste Land" for a class of rowdy, malodorous boys—something that had the puzzling effect of their imploring me to recite the poem again and again—Panic landed on her shoulder and whispered that, while she was in the library slogging for her exams on the art of the tragedy, I was mounting some mistress I'd arranged to meet in a cheap hotel room. At night, in tears, she confessed her anxiety, describing what she imagined, how I savagely and passionately made love to other women, how the music of my animal groans rang in some stranger's ears, my intoxicating musk inhaled by a rival. She went on and on about the girlfriends with whom I'd done it, and how I'd done it, and what I'd whispered during lovemaking, and wondered if I gave them the same caresses, kisses, licks, and bites I gave to her, but if I made the mistake of answering honestly, or if some tenderness crept unnoticed into my pronunciation of a previous lover's name—Shirley—she let out a yelp and covered her ears. She said she knew that jealousy was dreadful, but she was sure every woman went weak at the knees as soon as they saw me and—because of that desire and longing—could think of only one thing: sex, and being violated by me.

She was sweating over preparations for her final exams and came home exhausted every evening, her right hand—unaccustomed to so much writing—painfully cramped. I picked herbs in the meadows and brewed an infusion to massage into her hand and shoulders each night. To help her remember the key figures in the various periods of English literature, I drew a row of pillars on a large sheet of paper and wrote down names and dates, a well-known mnemonic device.

We still had a few months to prepare for our emigration to America, but now and then we looked at our possessions with an eye to the move.

Did we need to take this or that? Of course my plaster death mask of Beethoven was not up for discussion, but her terra-cotta head was another matter. The sculpted head had been made by some classmate of hers and served as a bookend. It was an ugly thing with the indifferent eyes of a prehistoric reptile—her features were barely recognizable. We didn't need it, she bravely said, but when I proposed smashing it to smithereens, she looked at me as if I'd suggested crushing her real head. We decided to find it a good home somewhere outdoors and went in search of a natural niche or pedestal along the banks of the Cam. She seemed nervous, unable to decide if she should laugh or cry. She said it was as if we were sacrificing something of herself to the gods, a sinister ritual to get rid of a shadow self, a copy in clay into which the evil part of her soul had been poured. But she also harbored a primitive fear that somebody would find the head and acquire power over her thoughts. While laying bare her fears, she reached up to the plait on her crown and said she felt a stab in her brain. To calm her, I told her about some tribes whose members craft a doll or head to represent themselves, which they then hide far from their huts so as to mislead the angry spirits with a false self and protect their genuine heads from evil invasions.

We found an ideal niche in the trunk of a willow tree, the perfect size, high enough to provide protection from the destructive impulses of young vandals and deep enough to shield it from pecking birds. I secured it firmly with some branches so it wouldn't fall into the river, performed a gracious bow before the shrine of her stone doppelgänger, and walked home arm in arm with the warm-blooded original.

In the weeks that followed, plagued by nightmares and blinding migraines, she tried to curb her fears by writing a poem, pored through *Roget's Thesaurus* to find as many synonyms as she could to represent reality, wrung the words "pastiche," "effigy," "copy," "imitation," "replica," "counterfeit," "image," and "simulacrum" into eight couplets, burst into tears when I called the poem artificial, and kept whittling away until five stanzas and four synonyms seemed sufficient to keep evil at bay.

Years after her death, condemned, hunted, and pursued by the worshippers of her totem, I returned to the spot where we'd left the head. With growing unrest, my eyes skimmed the banks of the Cam, as if the image would give me the key—some magic formula with which I could breathe new life into my ossified existence.

I searched for hours but could find no trace of the altar.

The closer we came to our departure date, the more she denigrated the country where she'd lived for two years, found a bridegroom, and completed her university education. The winters were harsh, the houses small, squalid, uncomfortable, and old, the people unkempt and unhygienic. Cambridge was a snake pit, and the literary world was suffocating and provincial. Single-minded, she sat before her Hermes typewriter each evening, venting her spleen in a novel she called *Falcon Yard* after the place where we had first met. It was intended to be both humorous and romantic, settling the score with former lovers—milksops—dealing with the years she'd spent at university among prisses, tomboys, and goody two-shoes, and showing how the quest of the self-destructive, desperate heroine—a femme fatale and Isis combined—is resolved through her true love for that special someone, a titan, a deceased creator resurrected in male form: companion, father, son, lover, and priest all rolled into one.

In other words, me.

Her desire to flee Europe and leave this grasping, colonial nation behind was intensified by England's imperialistic meddling in the Suez Crisis, coupled with the Hungarian Revolution. In America we'd find an island where we could both live, surrounded by nature, far from worldly squabbling. The rash on her arms—red tracks of interconnected blisters, her blood poisoned by compassion, fear, and loathing—was evidence of the sincerity of her abhorrence for the Russian invasion and the conflict in Gaza and of her empathy with those suffering peoples. She'd had a similar attack, she said, when the Rosenbergs were executed.

She'd won a writing competition in the summer of 1953 and was one of twenty women selected to spend a month in New York City, guest editing the high-heeled fashion magazine *Mademoiselle*. Along Fifth Avenue, headlines about the crime of the century shouted from every newsstand, billing the traitors' execution as not to be missed. It was the hot topic on the radio and all they talked about in the editing department. She read everything she could find about Julius and Ethel Rosenberg, a Jewish couple with two young children, accused of passing atomic secrets to the Communists, about Ethel's brother, who had betrayed Julius and his own sister. Above all—in a quasi-homeopathic effort to fight the horror by feeding it—she read as much as she could about the horrific death in the electric chair: how the sentence would be carried out, the strapping down, blindfolding, connecting the electrodes to the head, pulling the lever for two shots of two thousand volts—the most gruesome way a human could die. On the morning of June 19, the day of the execution, she went—sick and nauseous—down to the hotel's breakfast room. She couldn't stomach anything, and watched, retching, as the other girls tucked into their fully laden breakfast trays. Before she knew what was happening, she was on her feet, taking them to task. For God's sake, how could they eat at a time like this? Didn't they realize that in a little over an hour, the brains of a man and woman would be as fried as the eggs on their plates? She bolted from the indifferent masticators, walked out into hot and muggy New York, found some cool relief in a subway station, and sat on a bench, watching the clock. At the precise minute of their inhuman deaths—when the executioners carried out the scapegoats' sentences, terminating their lives and making orphans of two poor children—those very same rows of interconnected red blisters suddenly cropped up on her bare arms and began inching their way toward her heart.

Shortly after she graduated, in March 1957, one of her fairy godmothers pulled some strings so she'd be hired to teach English at Smith College. Everything was going our way. Our poems were appearing in print here and there, a British publisher wanted to release my award-winning poetry collection before the American edition appeared, and their editor—my literary hero, T. S. Eliot—had praised the work in a tribute that left me crowing with delight. The BBC broadcasts in which I read Yeats aloud became a hit with listeners, and the size of her salary at Smith was such that she proudly and generously offered to support us for a year so I could focus without distraction on my writing. I sputtered my dissent, but she confidently claimed her time would come—she was sure I'd become the greatest poet in England, but she would become the greatest poetess in America. She was certain of that.

We spent endless weeks packing possessions—a thousand pounds' worth, mostly books—into chests, trunks, and boxes, ready to set sail for America. We travelled to Heptonstall to say goodbye to my parents and relatives and to spend our last weeks in Europe with them. We'd also spent our first Christmas together at the Beacon, but back then we hardly took part in family life, something my sister—whom we'd put up just three weeks earlier in Cambridge—couldn't forgive, although she didn't seem to realize she was the main reason for our desire for privacy. During those Christmas holidays, my bride spent hours each day cramming for her exams, after which she wanted to go over the material with me alone so I could help her fill in the gaps in her grasp of literature. We had to ignore my unmarried sister's scornful looks when we came down the stairs, arms wrapped around each other, and headed out for long walks among the fields and hillocks. We didn't come home until it was time for supper.

On this occasion, however, without work as an excuse, and with our long-term absence in mind, we spent more time with my parents and my sister, who'd come over from Paris. We received my aunts and uncles and looked forward to a visit from Mr. Fisher, who would be coming to the Beacon with his wife to say goodbye to me and to meet my bride. She was a bundle of nerves about their arrival, especially since she knew how much I loved my old English teacher. She tried on five outfits, changed her hairstyle three times, and insisted on preparing an elaborate meal for the Fishers. Moody and on edge because she didn't have all the ingredients for her carefully orchestrated recipes at her fingertips, she was quaking like a hunted animal by the time the guests arrived. As usual when my bride was overwrought, she chattered her insecurities to shreds, was too fussy, too loud, too garish. The courtesy with which the Fishers hid their discomfort was as moving to me as her concerted efforts to make a good impression and win my approval. This divided loyalty resulted in my silence. All evening, I avoided my sister's eye. I looked at her only when she changed the subject, emphatically turning toward Mr. Fisher and inquiring about the well-being of a few of our mutual acquaintances from school, a topic clearly intended to silence her sister-in-law. At first, my bride was perplexed by this technical knockout, but after being excluded from the conversation for half an hour, she stood up and—with no apology—stormed out into the cold. When she hadn't returned after five minutes or so, I went looking for her. I found her cowering in the shed, offended, angry, and upset, and it took all my powers of persuasion to lure her back inside.

On June 20 we walked hand in hand up the gangplank of the *Queen Elizabeth* and leaned over the railing in a pleasurable Frieda and D. H. Lawrence manner until Southampton disappeared from view. Excited by the prospect of introducing me to her country, family, and friends, my homesick bride grew nostalgic and described the houses and locales of her youth, the sounds and smells of the ocean, the flowers, plants, and animals, and all the dishes I'd never tasted. I colored her descriptions in with snippets of Technicolor motion pictures, the only way I could imagine America. I had the Penguin paperback collection of

American poetry in my travel bag, a book that, through its extraordinary freedom and poetic daring, had paved the way for me to find my own voice, and reaffirmed the idea that life's struggles are not tied to one's place of birth, but are universal. I was looking forward to America as much as she was and was therefore perplexed by the depression that descended the first day we sailed, settling on top of me like an immovable hulking animal. I don't know if it was the agonizing slowness of the ship—after hours of sailing, the South Coast of Ireland was still visible—or the celebrated vastness of the ocean which offered me no challenge, no matter how authentically natural it was, but it bored me to tears and left me missing nature. Perhaps I simply felt cooped up, a prisoner on a boat, my only distraction three five-course meals a day and, in the evenings, a film in the ship's cinema. On the last night of our voyage, I spent hours holding a vomiting bride over the toilet. She only had to think of a blood-rare steak to throw up almost all the previous week's five-course meals. When, the next day, we approached New York—an unforgettably iconic moment for anyone who's ever arrived, fleeing some freedom-robber or other, thanks to the Statue of Liberty's stirring bravura, immense size, and symbolism—she was so weak I had to clasp her firmly to keep her knees from buckling. She collapsed anyway when we reached customs, a stern gorilla in uniform ordering her to open one of the trunks. He triumphantly plucked out *Lady Chatterley's Lover*, waved the book menacingly under her nose, and demanded to know why she was in possession of pornography.

"I'm going to be teaching it," she sniffed.

What was I expecting from the promised land? To be honest, everything. Everything that was novel or would make us new. The journey from New York to her mother's house in Wellesley affirmed the country's vastness: the ocean's waves were higher, the trees broader, the cars bigger than any I had ever seen. The houses also offered a sampling of all things splendid and new, with gleaming chrome refrigerators, shining worktops, electric cookers, central heating, sparkling pots and pans. Nothing was corroded by the rust of history, the sheets on the beds were crackling white, the pillows plumped with down, everything smelled of synthetic detergent and ersatz nature. We had forgone a wedding and gratefully accepted Aurelia's offer to host a reception. The day after we arrived, the guests were expected in a tent in the back garden at five o'clock. It was as if all seventy had been gathered around the corner, waiting to stampede the garden on the dot of five. They greeted me one by one, each as friendly, curious, and admiring as the last—a peck on the cheek from the women, a friendly pat on the shoulder from the men. My exuberant bride dragged me from this one to that, introducing me proudly to family, friends, classmates, neighbors, and acquaintances, until—tired and overwhelmed—I found myself yearning for a quiet, stinking world empty of blaringly happy, polite, cleanly scrubbed people.

At first I was relieved to say goodbye to the hustle and bustle and retreat with my bride to Cape Cod for our American honeymoon. After we'd been guests in Wellesley for three days, her brother drove us away in a car stuffed with suitcases and boxes of books, two bicycles tied to a rack on the roof. The seven-week stay on the coast had been a wedding present from Aurelia. With a certain nonchalance—intended to reveal, with hidden pride, the generosity of the gift—my bride let slip the sum her mother had paid to rent the vacation house on Cape Cod. The exorbitant amount paralyzed me to such an extent that I wasn't capable of accomplishing anything that first month. I'd never before experienced the depressing effects on a child of a mother's apparent self-sacrifice, the nagging guilt made me both sorrowful and enraged. I felt obliged to be grateful and was left with no idea how to cope with the acrid bile the gift had unleashed in me. Because my fatherless bride was an old hand at the same polarization, my mirror reflex pulled us both down into a dark mood.

We didn't enjoy what others call a holiday. To her, a day that went undescribed was a day lost. Her work on the novel had stalled, and I couldn't figure out what was holding me back to the point where all I could manage was a little scribbling in a notebook. The temperature rose above 90 degrees every day. We biked to a little beach where we felt like we were alone, went swimming, lay in the sun, read. We were happy but an unfamiliar veil hung over our joy, something misty that kept us from being able to discern each other's contours, and no matter how we tried to break through the fog, nothing seemed to work. An imminent catastrophe came to our rescue, startling us like threatened animals and drawing us out of our dreary inertia. Her menstruation—she always referred to it as "the curse"—failed to materialize. Our paradiselike Adam and Eve goings-on had made us reckless, and we did it wherever and whenever we liked, even if she didn't happen to have her diaphragm handy to ensure—for the time being—our childless future. The panic grew every day that the blood stayed away. She could clearly picture our idyllic future disintegrating, our writing together and fame, devoured by a child whom—this was the crux of it—she would surely hate because he had upset the applecart, the planned order of first the books and the fame, and then the babies and the champagne. Now, all that was out of the question—we were too poor to support a family, debt would pile up, I'd be forced to look for a job just as I was making a name for myself and success was within reach. She cried, hardly slept, gnawed her lips. I tried to calm her down, used hypnosis to bring on menstruation, but my own fear of a pregnancy was supplanted by a swollen jaw, an infection that had begun in my right ear, turning me half-deaf and making me look like the first chipmunk I'd ever seen—glimpsed a few days before all hell broke loose—a furry elf in a striped suit, cheeks rounded with stored acorns and nuts. He stared at me with beady, intelligent eyes, and my heart filled with joy until I suddenly saw myself from his perspective, a poet whose throat was clamped shut by his disgust at the stainless-steel world of abundance and falseness. For a moment it was as if I were looking into the eyes of my miserable bride, and every ounce of that ink-black gaze begged me to care for her forever.

It was a false alarm, and we celebrated with a bottle of chilled white wine and some lobster rolls. We drank to the curse, to the preservation of our ideal future—a life dedicated to poetry—and the sale of one of my poems to the *New Yorker*, the highest attainable honor, the bastion at the summit of a hierarchy, which she'd continually stormed with our poetry like a proud warrior. But I was of two minds. It was my first encounter with the untrustworthy side of fame. The poem that the *New Yorker* now praised had been rejected less than a year earlier by the selfsame editors, returned because they considered it unsuitable for publication. Thanks to my winning the First Publication Award and having the backing of a powerful publisher like Harper, the critics had changed their tune, afraid to miss out on a winner. What did this acceptance and sudden praise have to do with my work? My bride was so horrified by my contempt for shameless journalistic opportunism and its lack of independent judgment that I allowed myself to be muzzled by her sweet lament now that I'd accomplished all the things she'd longed for her entire life.

Less than twenty-four hours later, the first collection of poems she submitted to the celebrated Yale Series of Younger Poets landed back in our letter box, rejected.

From the moment I acquired renown as a poet, I've hated the public life that clings to it like a devil's tail. Why they call it a life is beyond me, it's more like the theft of life. The minute your name starts to echo in the world as an independent entity, torn from your body, your genuine existence, your raw reality and true personality, it gathers a significance that has nothing to do with you. Your disembodied name robs you of your freedom. It cages and imprisons you. When I was just starting out as a poet, I toyed with the idea of creating alternative literary personalities, as Pessoa did—I imagined a Daniel, a Peter—until I realized it was futile and would only stand in the way of what I was striving for: being a man of one piece. The freedom a pseudonym may grant you in public can't make up for the fragmentation of your inner self.

She told me a similar tale, but with a slight twist. During the years she referred to as her golden age—between seventeen and twenty, when she won prize after prize and saw everything that flowed from her pen published and praised—she participated in a poetry competition in two guises, using both her own name and a pseudonym. She won the first prize, her invented self the second.

"I was once a genius," she joked bitterly.

At the end of August, with mixed feelings, we left Cape Cod with its scents of sea, shellfish, and pine trees. She was overcome with guilt because, according to her inner Teutonic slave driver, she hadn't accomplished anything—she'd only managed to plow through the complete works of Virginia Woolf, D. H. Lawrence, Hawthorne, and Henry James to create teaching materials. I was leaving with nothing in my backpack but some children's stories and the first positive reviews of my poems. Our existence in that house by the sea had, for a brief time, resembled normal life, one that wasn't dictated by poetry, but to my bride, nothing could be just pleasurable anymore, everything had to be rewarded with success. The only exceptions to these Protestant economics were food and sex, which were rewards in themselves.

We moved into an apartment near Smith College in Northampton surrounded by woodland, and there we displayed our gleaming wedding presents, arranged our familiar books on the shelves, turned off the air-conditioning, and welcomed ourselves home with Beethoven's *Grosse Fuge* blaring from the record player. I'm not sure I completely fathomed just which spirits we were trying to dispel with the key of B-flat major, or how terrified she was of her new position, how much she was dreading exposing herself—only recently freed of student status herself—to the cold, frog-eyed stare of dozens of freshmen, pretending to be something she had yet to become, namely an adult, with no idea which corners in her character she had to conjure that up from.

On the Monday morning she was to give her first lecture, she sat petrified at the table, pale as death, her scar violet and throbbing with terror, in a mad blue flannel suit, her plaited hair like a helmet on her tiny skull. She clutched a mug of steaming Nescafé—the percolator coffee I'd made using our wedding present was too strong, and the milk, warmed in our brand-new stainless-steel pan, had boiled over. I must have sensed something of her anxiety, even though I had underestimated her fears. Looking at my bride, dressed as a teacher, she suddenly reminded me of her mother. I kept that to myself because it was the last thing she needed to hear. But perhaps it was running through her mind that morning as well. She felt, in her lonely misery, like her mother—a well-read, intelligent woman forced to accept work beneath her capabilities, sacrificing her talent and freedom to pay off the debt to everyone who had helped her get an education, working herself to the bone as a secretary in the service of a scribbling husband.

I never forgot the portrait she once sketched of Aurelia's surreptitious behavior, the fear it betrayed of puritanical Otto, how, as a much younger spouse, her mother had felt imprisoned by his entomological ambition to produce the standard reference work on the subject of bees. Whenever she wanted to relax with the girls, was in the mood for the type of company her husband didn't care for, she cunningly planned a dinner on his teaching night so as to be sure he wouldn't return home before ten. The dining table was always covered with notes, books, research materials, and pages of his manuscript she'd typed and corrected herself, so she made a map of its surface, carefully noted the order and angle of everything, and only then cleared the table to welcome her forbidden guests. She managed to shoo her visitors out the door before he came home and, using her drawing, put everything back exactly as it had been before he'd left.

My bride had just turned eight when her father died as a result of neglecting his diabetes. She was furious because it had been an unnecessary death, leaving her mother a widow and her and Warren without a father. By 1940, insulin had ensured that no one need die of diabetes, but he'd interpreted his ailments as symptoms of terminal lung cancer, from which a colleague had recently died, and so, with an obstinate fatalism, he hid his lonely march to what he thought was a certain death. He consulted a doctor only when his deterioration became impossible to ignore. By then, the diabetes had ravaged his body to such an extent that a blackened leg had to be sawn off. According to Aurelia, her daughter had then asked if Daddy still needed to buy shoes in pairs, because now of course he only needed one. The anecdote irritated her no end, along with the way her mother used this often-repeated twaddle to abort the reality within her eight-year-old soul. Whenever she had the opportunity, Aurelia recounted with similar pride the first words her young smarty-pants had said when, a month after the amputation, she sat at her daughter's bedside to tell her that her daddy had died. "I'm never going to speak to God again," my bride had said. Just eight.

In reality she was pursued by atrocious fantasies of bloody amputations, limbs crushed and burned, stoked like garbage in a hospital furnace. She had a growing fear that, in a wave of pity for her mother, who was working her fingers to the bone, she had wished so often for the death of her adored and cursed father that a forthright God—who understood nothing of the whims of children—had been insane enough to answer her prayers.

The only way of introducing my fatherless bride to her daddy was by charting his horoscope. I did it with gritted teeth, because I was getting fed up with her complaining about being unable to calculate the aspects herself. Whenever she struggled with her syntax; exclaimed with growing panic that the novel wasn't going well, that poetry had turned against her; or felt she was locked inside a bell jar while a brilliant book, a bestseller, was outside tapping impatiently on the glass, beyond reach, then I'd tell her to look at the shadow planet in her star sign, her Pisces ascendant, which continually obstructed and dragged down every talent she had. It was a metaphor of course, but who understands that kind of thing? Depending on her mood—curious or skeptical—she would ask when Mr. Saturn would stop blocking her way.

"As soon as you've learned to understand a little more about yourself," I'd snarl.

I could only be approximate when drawing up her father's horoscope. She knew he'd been born early in the morning of April 13—a day I later saw described in her journal as her salvation day, the same Friday the thirteenth I took her father's place—but she didn't know the exact time, so I couldn't chart that Aries ascendant precisely. As I drew, the heavens under which Otto Plath had come into the world gradually appeared. He was born at the end of the nineteenth century in a small East Prussian city. She was leaning against me, nervously twisting a lock of her fringe. When I grunted from time to time because I'd noticed a peculiar conjunction or an astonishing alignment with her stars, she impatiently asked what I'd seen, or should I say *whom* I'd seen, because by drawing his chart, I was bringing her father to life and getting to know him—enviably—somewhat before she could. A portrait emerged from these aspects, houses and ruling planets of an extremely nervous perfectionist: rigid, mistrustful, authoritarian, obstinate, extraordinarily intelligent, and yet unable to forge strong bonds with others. I was baffled as to why he'd taught biology and German at various institutions, because according to his horoscope, he was completely unsuited to teaching. What didn't surprise me was that he'd lost his inheritance because of Darwin. Aurelia had related the story with a certain pride, one of the rare occasions when she showed any sign of tenderness for her unapproachable spouse. After he'd moved to America as a fifteen-year-old boy, he was supported by his grandparents, who'd made the journey earlier, on the condition that their grandson attend the Lutheran seminary and become a minister. While at the seminary, he secretly read Darwin's *Origin of Species* and decided to walk out on his studies. He was then disinherited and excommunicated. His grandfather opened the family Bible, as he stood watching, and doggedly crossed out his name. I felt a glimmer of unreserved sympathy for the man whose almighty, ubiquitous absence had colored my bride's life and my own destiny. The other anecdote that amused and confused me was one Aurelia knew from hearsay, a story going around campus before she had started taking his class as a student of German. To confront the freshmen with their personal prejudices and conventional notions regarding nature, he would shock each new crop of biology students at the start of the academic year by skinning a dead rat in front of the class, roasting it, and savoring it on the spot, thereby challenging, with a full mouth, their blinkered perceptions.

I later discovered a link between the two things my bride said she dearly wanted to learn but which remained stubbornly out of reach. The reason she seemed unable to master German or draw up a horoscope, despite her intelligence, was, as I later understood, that she had no desire to speak the language of her father or that of her bridegroom, because both languages demanded she delve deeper into herself.

Everything that's denied and repressed, every conflict that's swept under the carpet and disavowed, in a culture or in an individual's existence, seeks a way out and ultimately—violent, destructive, diabolically disguised—turns against life.

I've often been accused of glorifying violence in my poetry, but it's a misreading that betrays an appalling lack of understanding. After my bride's suicide, the scribes—especially the feminists among them—used this false attribution as an excuse to call me a fascist, sadist, tyrant, vampire, male oppressor, even a murderer. What they see as atrocious and abhorrent in my poems are qualities they do not wish to see in nature, in our so-called civilized culture, and especially not in themselves. All great literature—Homer, Dante, Shakespeare, Blake, the Bible—is about the struggle with the forces of evil, against something that—inside us and out—is hell-bent on our destruction, the death of the body or the soul.

To deny violence is to summon it.

To deny evil is to summon it.

In all my stories and poems, the denial of the evil lurking within us is the source of all misery, and insight and knowledge then become the salvation. Evil can be used to create something good through understanding, ordering, and ritualization. That's what literature and religion are for.

As pleasant and light as the apartment on Elm Street was, it's one of the few addresses I have difficulty calling to mind, as if the memories have to traverse an abyss to reach me. The windows at the back looked out on a well-manicured park full of catalpa trees, rhododendrons, rosebushes, azaleas, squirrels, rabbits, and chirping birds, but they could hardly drown out the traffic noise from the street. Outside, it stank of exhaust fumes, and the racket during recess from a nearby school surpassed the decibel levels from the planes flying overhead. My uniformed bride left for Smith every morning, stressed and depleted, and I spent the day staring apathetically at an empty sheet of paper. She cycled home at lunchtime because, in her own words, she could manage only so many hours without hearing, touching, and smelling me. I waited for her with lunch ready and, grinning, allowed her to have a good sniff. Wiped out, bone-weary, and unhappy, she couldn't conceal her hatred of teaching. I became febrile and distant, kept quiet about how paralyzed I was by the generous sacrifice of her time, and how American life was too impenetrable for me to wring any meaning out of it at all.

The new world was literally too new.

In England, every hill, shrub, and tree sang an ancient ballad; the moorland, houses, and rivers whispered folktales about witches and spirits in my ear, and I saw Scrooges, Shylocks, and Clarissas strolling through the city streets, but the small-town life of Northampton didn't conjure any association; it seemed as though no history could take root in that leveled earth, and everything that was dark and perishable suffocated under a galvanized coating. I felt like a prisoner, although of what, I did not know. That was also the first house in which we didn't write together every day, sometimes back-to-back, sometimes at opposite ends of the same table. It hadn't occurred to me then.

It does now.

What in England had sounded like a lavish salary turned out in America to be hardly enough to pay the bills each month. The specter of getting stuck in America because we lacked the funds for a return to Europe spurred me to take a job as well, and from the start of 1958, I taught English and creative writing classes at the University of Massachusetts. We were both alarmed by our transformation into an average teaching couple, working during the day, living for the weekends and holidays, and only free to do what we really wanted in the time that was left. We corrected students' tests and essays, held dinner parties for colleagues, opened a savings account, walked through the park in the evenings, and, shortly before celebrating our second anniversary, had an enormous row.

One of her colleagues at Smith—an Englishman—had translated *Oedipus Rex*. We'd invited him and his wife to dinner, and he asked if I would take the role of Creon during a public reading of the work, intended to conclude the academic year. I could hardly say no, but regretted the obligation because I detest acting. We rehearsed the skillfully translated Sophocles with a couple of colleagues, and, on the day before our performance, I begged my bride to stay home the following night, to not waste her time listening to my tin-eared bumbling.

The next night, while I was plodding through my lines in front of a packed auditorium, I spied her slipping in through the back door, just at the end of this cringe-making display. My anger and shame took my breath away to the extent that I screwed up the tragic denouement, barely able to sputter Creon's judgment to Oedipus—played by an English professor of the worst kind. I managed to put a little more vigor into the closing line, accepted the applause with the rest of the cast, and bolted from the stage. We were led to a back room, where we congratulated ourselves and, satisfied, drank some wine. The two glasses I gulped down weren't enough to dispel my mortification, so I sat at the piano to withdraw from the company and hammered out some inane tune until my bride entered.

I couldn't face her.

I was fed up with the suspicion that had driven her to the theater, and felt humiliated by my performance and the paltry troupe I had joined. I didn't belong here, and I didn't want to belong. An hour later, we walked home in silence. Before we went to bed, she made an effort to lighten the mood by asking what was bothering me.

I said nothing.

The next morning, we should have been happy and relieved. She'd valiantly turned down the school's offer of a contract for a second year, even though in so doing, she left herself wide open to the incessant griping of her mother, colleagues, and benefactresses about status, a steady paycheck, responsibility, and social security. She was tired of meat-and-potatoes thinking, as she described the mind-numbing effect of teaching. I had already finished my work at the university, and she just needed to say goodbye to her three classes and then correct the final exams. We had planned to celebrate our renewed freedom to devote ourselves wholeheartedly to poetry. I said I'd wait for her on campus. But I was still in a foul mood and hadn't paid attention to the where and when.

We got our wires crossed, she went looking for me, and saw me with a young coed who'd taken my creative writing class in Boston, a lass who—with fawning blandishments—was telling me how much she'd enjoyed my Creon, and, flattered by the attention, I may have bestowed a friendly smile on her—I'm no longer certain—but the grin was soon wiped off my face by the approach of my bride's hailstone eyes, causing the sweet young thing to flee and me to parry coldly.

What followed was a week of staccato mortar fire, dredged-up suspicions about the times I came home late with some excuse or other, how she knew in her gut I was cheating on her, that I'd transformed her from a friendly creature into a misanthrope by teaching her to be what I called "real and genuine," that our university clique didn't deserve her unbridled human kindness—but now she'd caught me red-handed with that backward wench, the simpering grin I'd given that empty-headed slut made her sick to her stomach. I was every bit as vain as all the other ugly, promiscuous, despicable arseholes at Smith who cheated on their wives with students, taken in by the brainless adoration of dim-witted teenyboppers, and I was no better than all the others, just another cowardly, underhanded, egotistical, adulterous, conceited liar. She would have done anything for me, but now that she'd lost me and the house stank of infidelity and lies, she couldn't feel any love, only disgust and hate.

I thought it pointless to repeat what I'd already said—that I'd been looking for her on campus, had forgotten where and when we'd agreed to meet, and that the girl was a student whose name I didn't know for sure, maybe Shirley or Sheila.

So I kept my mouth shut.

I was silent for seven days, stoically listening to the reproaches, sleeping like a baby every night while she became more and more haggard. I was almost relieved when, on the eighth day, she pounced on me like a panther, scratching my face and almost biting off my ear. I pushed her away with half a laugh. She came at me again, fuming with rage, hissing like a savage, and choking with frenzy. It must have been something I'd picked up from a film, but I could think of no way of bringing her to her senses other than slapping her in the face. She spun around, astonished, and I—afraid I'd brought her down—came to her aid, caught my falling angel, pressed her to me, and, a moment later, heard a relieved giggling that soon morphed into soft and gentle weeping.

Fame arrived, and that made no one happier than my bride. My debut collection attracted favorable reviews. I admired the tone of the American critics: witty, intelligent, erudite, and objective, quite a change from the admittedly positive but stodgy English reviews in which one of their own poets was cautiously held up against some trusted yardstick, in fear of sounding the trumpet too early for something new and controversial. I was particularly proud of the critique written by W. S. Merwin for the *New York Review of Books*. He was one of the poets I'd become acquainted with through my Penguin paperback, and I admired him. I was invited to give a talk at Harvard, enjoyed watching my wife dab away a tear in the front row, was introduced to writers I knew only by name, and gratefully accepted an invitation from the dean to dine at his house with William Merwin and his wife, Dido, who was fifteen years his senior and an English aristocrat.

No matter how intimidated I may have been during our first encounter, this faun-like man soon won me over with his good-hearted yet amused gaze. It was the first time I'd met someone in the US with whom I could form a friendship. He seemed to share my interest in nature, the zodiac, myths. He knew Robert Graves personally—had been his son's teacher in Mallorca—his first poetry collection had won a prize coveted by my bride, and he was blessed with the good looks of a film star and the wisdom of a shaman. It was only somewhat later, when I met the artist Leonard Baskin and recognized in him a rabbinical mentor and kindred spirit, that I realized how much I missed my friends.

A few weeks before our move to Boston, on a mild summer evening, we took a stroll through the park. She clipped a rose for the bud vase at home, something she often did. She never carried out this theft without first apologizing to the shrub, the park, and even to the whole country, an adorable courtesy that always left me beaming, but the evening of the incident, her politeness had the opposite effect, leading to an unpleasant encounter. She'd just stolen a rose, excused her behavior with a contrite bow to the bush, thereby obtaining moral carte blanche for having committed this petty crime, when we heard the excited voices of a group of young girls and saw a rhododendron bush being shaken violently. My bride gave me the look I knew well—fixed, icy, and deadly. She strode over to the three young ladies, still clutching her rose, and stood sentry beside the rhododendron, trying to turn the spritely elves to stone with her Medusa-like glare and halt the vicious theft of half the rhododendron's branches. The girls paid no attention to my vengeful fury's disapproving demeanor. I made some half-hearted remark about senseless destruction of property, put my arm around her shoulders, which were trembling with rage, and led her from the scene. She was so upset I didn't dare ask what had triggered her killer instinct. When she was in one of her moods, her extreme behavior usually aroused both my awe and my urge to protect her. A few days later, when she read me a poem in which she'd transformed the trifling event into a poetic fable, I still didn't make the connection.

Three years later—when, in a span of just six weeks, she focused all her plutonic energy on writing the novel that would posthumously bring her the fame she'd longed for in life—I read the scene about her visit to her father's grave. Only then did my blood run cold. The passage recalled the incident with the rhododendron, and I finally realized that the killer instinct wasn't directed at the girls, but at herself. In it, she describes how one drab, rainy day Esther Greenwood—her alter ego—visits the Azalea Path in the cemetery just outside Winthrop to look for her father's grave. She plucks a large bunch of azaleas from a shrub near the fence at the entrance. She places the stolen salute on the headstone, a full two fathoms beneath which her father lies, and cries for him for the first time in her life. In the following paragraph, she descends the stairs into the basement with a bottle of sleeping pills, worms her way into the crawl space, and attempts to follow her father in death.

I was there when she visited the grave. We were living in Boston, and yes, it was raining. She bought a bunch of flowers at a stall around the corner from our house. Red roses, if memory serves.

Success arrived complete with invitations to festivals, parties, receptions, and dinners, where I rubbed shoulders with renowned poets, icons of literature, smug and sacrosanct, who were enjoying their many years of consolidated fame. This was their habitat, and they behaved as if they'd grown accustomed to other guests gawking at them when they arrived, scurrying over with glasses of champagne and tarted-up mistresses, armed with amusing or quasi-intelligent questions or anecdotes prepared in advance.

The only way I could entertain myself during such gatherings was to observe the scene as if I were a scientist examining an exotic biotope. The pecking order, the pandering, flattering, kowtowing of the lackeys, the courtship displays, the mimicry. It was also the only way of maintaining a safe distance, to keep from becoming infected with the contagious virus every inhabitant carried in their colorful plumage: a longing for admiration.

Writers don't belong in a pack. They're too solitary, too egoistic, too proud for that. They thrive on isolation. What's more, they're so in love with their own workmanship that they view their contemporaries' creations with a slight antipathy. No matter how successful or well known other poets may become, writers still find their own work more authentic, sharp-witted, bold. This threatens to become a problem only when the writer longs for others to share his solipsistic opinion, when he desires the praise of epigones, scribes, and pharisees who form a ring around the literary world's trunk and feed like bracket fungus on the sap of its bark. The more chance a writer gives the outside world to penetrate his secluded existence, the more he exposes his true self to the danger of being corrupted and, ultimately, destroyed. But a social life's demands, commitments, and temptations pale in comparison with the threats from within, those of the dark forces intent on destroying all that's sacred within one's self.

I became acquainted with those forces the day I met her. I thought they came from her, my white goddess, my fainthearted muse, and that I could protect her from harm. But instead, I met my own demons in the guise of a woman.

Wring its neck, I suggested, something my brother and I used to do when we were children, but she thought that was a gruesome idea. Gas would be the kindest death. We'd spent the week caring for a little bird that had fallen out of its nest. We took it home and, like proud parents, spent hours stooped over the box of twigs we'd placed it in. We fed it chopped beef, worms, and morsels of soggy bread, woke up at night when we heard its restless scrabbling, and took turns looking after the sickly newborn, staring at the gasping rib cage, caressing the minuscule downy skull with the tip of a little finger, full of wonder at its desperate will to stay alive. When we found it one morning exhausted from its struggle, gasping for breath, its beak agape, the frail wings paralyzed under a layer of caked-on droppings, lacking the strength to stand up, we decided to put it out of its misery. And that's when she said that gas is the kindest death for any living being. While I was in the kitchen, piping gas from the oven into the box, she hid wailing behind the bed, as if she could block out the image of the dying bird. She didn't calm down until she saw how death had brought it peace, and even noticed the hint of a smile around its beak that hadn't been there before.

We relocated to Boston in the autumn of 1958, to an address that seemed to have chosen us. Some months before we moved into 9 Willow Street, I'd paid a visit to the barber. There—tired of looking at my own reflection—I flipped through a magazine in which I saw a picture of a street on Beacon Hill, an older neighborhood in Boston where Henry James's characters had lived. That—together with his reminiscences about history, plus the sweet recollection of the name of the house where I grew up—aroused and assuaged my homesickness. With a feeling of excited premonition—might as easily have been hope playing a sly masquerade—I knew that my bride and I would find some accommodation there. The realtor thought our chances were slim, but in September we were nevertheless climbing up the stairs to our minuscule fifth-floor Beacon Hill apartment, with a view over the rooftops and, to the west, the Charles River. The street I'd seen in the photograph was just opposite.

The address was full of promise for any poet, Cabalist, or fortune-teller. But I had discovered that my bride had been slowed down and made inert by blackest Saturn, while the same planet, wonder of wonders, had brought me happiness. Her stars must have been stronger, or her ballast heavier, because from the start, the willow refused to rock us, and that sacred number offered the muses no place to rest their heads. We'd both had such high hopes for the prospect of freedom, the endless sea of time following a year spent smothering the voices of our souls with teaching and wage earning. For months on end we'd told ourselves: this is only temporary. In June, as soon as we'd put the humdrum existence of alarm clocks and obligations behind us, all barriers would disappear, and the ideas and sentences would flow freely.

Not quite.

For the first time in her life, my bride found herself outside the walls of a school or university and had to do without the starring role as a brilliant student or passionate instructor, without the lurid heroism of the young woman who'd survived suicide. The week's plans weren't dictated by a lesson schedule or seminars, and all at once the free time she'd so been looking forward to was leering at her like a monster. It was only then that her inner tyrant proved to be a harsher despot than the cruelest dictator in the outside world. Every Monday morning—those eternal Mondays—a fresh list would appear beside her Hermes typewriter, on which, with furious underlining and exclamation marks, she gave herself assignments for the coming week, all beginning with the imperative: I must. I must learn German, I must write a bestseller, I must finish a story completely, I must read *On the Origin of Species*, I must study Shakespeare, I must produce a collection of poems, I must fight my vanity, I must not shirk my responsibilities, I must, I must, I must.

Sometimes—weary from that choking impotence—I said she must let go of the idea of a bestseller, at least end her obsession with publishing, magazines, and success; that she must push away the outside world and concentrate on herself, discover the inner urgency driving her work.

"I hate the word 'must,'" she said.

"If only that were true," I answered.

In between our departure from Northampton and the move to Boston, we spent a week in New York—the only parts I liked were the fringes of Manhattan, because those were the only places I could breathe. The views there revealed the horizon otherwise hidden by skyscrapers, light came from the sun and not from some glaring neon advertisement, and the calming fragrance of water replaced the hectic exhaust fumes in the streets and avenues. The *New Yorker* had for the first time accepted two of her poems, something that left her feeling like a victor who'd conquered the entire metropolis. We walked for hours and wherever possible avoided travelling in the belly of the city, in that intestinal system of connections, crammed on top of each other among the city's residents, hiding behind a newspaper or book, avoiding any form of eye contact.

We'd recently seen Marianne Moore at a poetry festival in Boston. While reading, she kept butchering her own poems by adding asides, something that had a quaint effect and didn't seem to bother her admiring audience. My bride had met her some years earlier when, as a student, she'd participated in a poetry competition for which Moore was a jury member. Although she won joint first prize, she could still hear Moore's critical remarks as if they'd been pronounced yesterday. The grand old lady of American poetry advised the young poets to find undemanding jobs so they could devote their evenings and weekends to writing. In her remarks about my wife's contribution, she said she found the use of adjectives excessive to the point of mannerism.

In Boston she came face-to-face with her critic again and introduced me to the woman who may well have been responsible for the publication of my first poetry collection, but was nevertheless someone I approached with mixed feelings. She'd had some hesitation about awarding the prize to *The Hawk in the Rain*. She had requested—or rather, demanded—that three of the poems be removed and replaced. Although she gave no reason for her veto, it clearly had to do with the poems' explicit sexual content. At first I was piqued and wrote to the commission to say the sexuality was an undeniable part of my poetic view of nature, but in the end I yielded and selected three alternative poems, afraid of missing out on the award.

I regret it to this day.

When we saw her in Boston, she'd invited us to visit her when we were in New York, and now, her address in hand, we were walking across the Brooklyn Bridge. My bride was curious and excited because she'd always hoped to pick up some tips from the woman who had held her own for more than half a century in the male-dominated world of literature. She swallowed her secret disdain for spinsters, for untouched bodies, clearly never warmed by a hunger for passion, for the lives of women falling short of their full potential by failing to become the lover and muse of a husband or the mother of a child.

Our elderly poetess awaited us at the top of a narrow staircase and led us like a hopping bowerbird into her nest, a tiny room stuffed full of porcelain bric-a-brac and shiny knickknacks, where, reclining in an overstuffed chintz armchair, she chirped incessantly about friends and fellow poets, legendary encounters, a long life devoted to poetry, and her enthusiasm for young talent. She then complimented me personally on my poetry collection, which she had chosen above all others, enumerated its strong points, and failed to say a single word about the work of my bride. I was feeling more uncomfortable by the minute, but that wasn't the only reason. I abhorred the power she displayed, bold as brass—cunningly disguised as historical anecdotes. Or perhaps I loathed what it did to me.

I've lost count of how many people I have met who, one way or another, influence how our work is received. Poets who sit on committees allocating subsidies and grants, who take part in juries and decide who will be acclaimed or rejected, who use a job as editor or critic to keep their heads above water while submerging ours, who have the power to determine the fate of others. I'm repulsed by the idea that I have to be friendly for those reasons. In fact, it often makes me appear less amicable than I truly am, and I approach representatives of judgmental power with more foot-dragging and stubbornness than I do people I really despise. I take such pains to repress anything that might resemble hypocrisy or groveling that I sometimes have no idea who I'm talking to. I'm penalized by days of melancholy for every second I betray myself during an encounter with some literary potentate, laugh about a story that bores me to tears, or hide my fault-finding when it comes to a body of work that everyone else seems to adore.

Miss Moore was a member of practically every committee and jury in the land. A few weeks after our visit, my bride mailed her the carbon copies of a few poems, along with a polite request for a letter of recommendation for a grant application. Glowing with expectation, she ripped open the envelope on which Moore's cursive handwriting betrayed her nineteenth-century mastery of the Palmer method. A short while later she was on the floor like a beaten dog, weeping in astonishment about the blow she'd been dealt. Moore's rejection was malicious, humiliating, self-satisfied, cynical, and arrogant. She seemed particularly indignant about having received mere carbon copies of the poems, which she scornfully returned.

From then on, I hated the old bag and banished her to the third ring of Dante's *Inferno*. Five years after the suicide, I saw her again when she was visiting the United Kingdom. She was holding court, surrounded by followers, wearing a ridiculous arty hat with a floppy brim to cover her thinning hair. She saw me among the guests and beckoned. All I could now do for my dead wife was approach the frayed old hypocrite without an indulgent smile, my eyes as cold as glass, the image of my defeated bride blazing behind my retina. It was bad enough I practically had to kneel to hear what she so urgently wanted me to know, but when she deigned with a flickering-sweet voice to misquote the title of my bride's last short story and to call the literary gem so wonderful, so enlightened, I could hardly disguise my repugnance for this posthumous homage. Morose, I accepted the compliment without a word and, with that, tried to remain faithful to my buried beloved.

As an apology, this quiet homage fell well short of the mark. When I stood up again, I felt like a collaborator who had willingly lent an ear to one of her tormentors.

I could hardly walk upright in our apartment on 9 Willow Street, although each of us did have our own workroom for the first time since we'd been married, and initially that seemed to increase our mutual clinginess. Her growing desperation seeped through the walls of the bedroom and on the other side, my darkening mood pushed her deeper into the muck. Everything I wrote was a struggle against the impossibility of writing, attempts to preserve something of myself or perhaps to rediscover who I was. When I first heard her sobbing in the next room, I went over to calm and comfort her, but it happened so often I gave up, put in earplugs, and only embraced her in bed at night, when we made dreary love and tried briefly to mislead death with our passion.

Driven by an ever-growing, oppressive fear of both poverty and the empty hours, and harassed by a mother who bombarded her with advice about learning shorthand—the world always needed secretaries who'd mastered it, as she had—she found a job in the same hospital where, five years earlier, she'd been admitted to the accompaniment of wailing sirens, half-comatose, escaping by a hair's breadth the desire to sacrifice herself like a lamb on the altar of love. She viewed her job on the psychiatric ward—where she typed up treatment reports—as a boon to her own work.

"I must get out of myself," she said.

I said nothing, didn't contradict her, let her go. It's difficult to admit—in retrospect—but I was happy to be alone for a few hours a day, free of her suffering like a flagellant under the weight of the holy "must," a flogging meant to beg mercy from a punishing God or an uncooperative muse, an unholy penance for a sin she hadn't committed. More and more often, I caught myself thinking she wasn't really in search of solace, that she was too attached to the pain to liberate herself from a familiar alliance with God the Father, a devouring mother, the delicious intensity of her panic, and the tempting release of death. And therefore had no use for me.

I'd cobbled a few planks together to make a table in the bay window of the bedroom and covered the lower half of the windows with paper to avoid the temptation of hours spent staring at the river. If I wasn't reading or scribbling—a children's story, a poem, a letter—I was lying on the bed and thinking of poetry and England. There was a strident contrast between the vitality of her fears and the slow, insidious anesthesia affecting all my senses, kept in a stranglehold by an enemy whose name I did not yet know. I hoped it was America, or homesickness, or even the weight of love, but the somber feeling was too familiar to entirely rule out the possibility that it was some dark thing within myself.

Relieved as I was every morning when she closed the door behind her, I was just as happy to hear her coming back up the stairs in the afternoon, delighted to see her animated face, to embrace her seemingly boneless body, to listen to the witty anecdotes about her encounters in the psychiatric clinic, the strange kinks of the spirit she'd observed as a secretary, reassuring her that, in fact, she was completely healthy and normal, even though she classified herself as a schizo with an IQ of 166, an Electra complex, penis envy, and a larger than average sexual appetite. We celebrated her twenty-sixth birthday on a pleasant autumn day in October. I'd asked her a week earlier what she wanted.

"Immortality," she said.

"It's yours," I said.

She started going on about children—ideally four or five—and even though I couldn't picture myself as a father, after her endless pleading,

I set aside my hesitation, tried to see fatherhood as riding the wave of nature's unrelenting course: man, woman, child. I'd be a terrific father, she insisted, because the way I wrote for children showed how much I empathized with their world. She could already picture me surrounded by our brood, illuminated by the hearth flames, reading fairy tales aloud in my sonorous voice, and making them shudder and tremble, as I made her shudder and tremble in bed when I told ghost stories. I didn't correct her misconception. The truth was I felt more like a boy when I was working on children's stories, a boy crouched on his haunches next to his brother beside a campfire and listening with bated breath to the exciting adventures of cowboys and Indians. Or at his mother's side, with her endless yarns about apparitions and epiphanies, and how, in the middle of the night, she was awoken by her dead sister, or by a burning pain in her heart when her brother committed suicide, or how an urge propelled her one night to the window, where she saw hundreds of small crucifixes, one after the other, flashing above the church's steeple—the following day she discovered that each and every cross represented someone from the valley who'd died, a soldier who hadn't survived the invasion of Normandy. To be honest, nothing was easier for me than writing such tales: exciting, dark, imaginative, able to give the listeners the same goose pimples I experienced as a boy—a marvelous sensation I tried, when alone, to re-create and foster by reading ghost stories, myths, and fairy tales. Once you see the angle, all these stories are variations on a theme, and making them up becomes child's play. However, my wife often became as envious of these unbridled fantasies as she was of my abundant dreams. I tried to temper her resentment by making clear that what everyone calls fantasy is really just a way of discovering universal truths, truths which return, century after century, in all their ghastliness, inexhaustible in their distortion of the same thing: the marital struggle between good and evil.

She stopped using her diaphragm and each month we counted the days, anxiously wondering if the curse would arrive. The first months

I was relieved each time it did, but the blood became a new sting of fear and loathing to my broody wife. She saw infertility as a greater failure than the inability to write a novel. She was afraid that during her deflowering by a physics professor—the hemorrhage that resulted had landed her in the emergency room—something had been damaged forever, and so we made an appointment with a doctor. The preliminary examination proved she was healthy as a horse and just needed to be patient. Most likely it was the nervous tension that had as yet prevented the merging of sperm and egg.

She cried every day, and it drove me little by little to the end of my tether. If I was feeling up to it, I tried to help her, I probed and diagnosed, consulted Jung, Freud, Cabala, the zodiac, and all the world's creation myths to try to understand in which labyrinth she had lost her way, to find out the names of her demons. Was she in a no-man's-land because of the lack of authority figures who expected something from her, offering a daily routine and prodding her ambition with demands to excel at everything? Was she—in America, in Boston, the city of her birth—too close to the past, to a living, nagging mother; a dead, demanding father; a bygone golden age; the suicide attempt? Was she, as a poet, in a transition phase, a period of chaos and paralysis she had to get through to find another voice, the voice of her real self, and was she shying away from that initiation, afraid of who she would encounter if she plumbed the depths of her psyche? Or was it us? Were we too bound up with each other so that even our moods had started to align, dragging each other down into the underworld?

I forget what her answers were. Like as not she said both yes and no to everything. After such talks, often lasting deep into the night, her mood would lift for a few days. The curl was back in her hair, she baked an ingenious cake every day and scrubbed the house from top to bottom. But as soon as she started whining that I must find a job, wash my hair, put on a clean shirt, manicure my fingernails; complained that I could cook too, at least sometimes; or called me a fanatical curmudgeon and started throwing all my old socks away, I knew we were back to square one.

To break the impasse, we made up our minds to return to England in December of 1959. To me, the decision came as a huge relief—an understatement, I was jumping for joy—and with the liberating prospect of the approaching end to what was starting to feel more and more like an exile, I thought I would probably be able to endure the next few months in America. In the meantime, my poems had been published for a tidy sum in various magazines in both England and America, I'd received a grant, we'd been invited for an eleven-week stay at the Yaddo artists' colony, and my tormented bride was secretly turning for help to Dr. Ruth Beuscher, the psychiatrist who had treated her in the loony bin after her suicide attempt.

We talk about our loved ones with others, sometimes in their presence, sometimes behind their backs, lauding or lamenting them, with affection or with the coolness of a temporary alienation. I've never talked much about my wife. During her life, I was silent to protect her from the preconceptions and misunderstandings of my friends; after her death, I was silent to protect myself from the idolizing preconceptions and misunderstandings of her followers. She was a paragon others could project their ideals onto, both during her lifetime and after her death, and her worshippers' image of her had nothing to do with the way I knew her, what she was like from one minute to the next, what it was like to be loved by her, to adore her, to be her husband, live with her. But being the husband of a spouse who is seeing a psychiatrist is something else entirely. You know you'll be the subject of discussion, that within the seclusion of an office you'll be fleshed out as one of the most important characters in her version of the story, which she'll be telling in the presence of a professional reader, qualified to interpret, to hear what's not being said, to endow the protagonist with hidden qualifications, to turn the prince back into a frog, to rob the gods of their halos, and to unmask devils as the incarnations of guilt, sorrow, fear, and resentment.

After two sessions she confessed that she had again placed herself in Dr. Beuscher's care. She'd been afraid I would feel sidelined, and of course we couldn't afford it, but for now Dr. Beuscher was treating her for free, and she felt she needed professional help, that she must put her heart into it—I'd said so myself—figure out where the panic attacks were coming from, why she was unable to write, why she was energetic and euphoric one minute, lethargic and downcast the next. She was at her wits' end with all the anxiety and nightmares, jealousy of her brother, dislike of her mother, grief for her father. She wanted to take the burden off my shoulders, because I was the one who had always listened patiently, comforted her, showed limitless understanding for her flaws. She had to become her own person, otherwise she'd ruin what we had, the most amazing marriage imaginable, and she was terrified that one day I'd be fed up with all that crying and whining without making any headway. She wanted to be a good wife to me and a loving mother to our children, but she was also a writer; she knew that a brilliant poetess was trapped inside her, and if she couldn't free her, she would destroy our lives.

I wanted nothing more than for her to find help, for Dr. Beuscher to succeed where I had failed, felt relieved she was looking for the source of her anxieties with someone else, and had to accept that, in the mind of an unfamiliar woman, I would become a character beyond my own control. My bride went to considerable lengths to let nothing slip about her sessions, and I didn't pry. The only clue that I'd been the subject of discussion was when she followed her analyst's advice by altering her behavior. Every morning I brought her a glass of fresh orange juice in bed, crawled back under the covers once she'd got up, and when I finally arose, I'd find the kitchen table set for breakfast. One morning, the table was empty. No problem. It was only when I caught her surreptitiously stuffing a typescript into an envelope that I became uneasy. I asked what it was.

"A story," she said offhandedly.

It was the first time she'd sent something into the world without asking me to read it first. I found the story, "Johnny Panic," after she died, among an immense pile of typescripts and manuscripts she'd left behind as a lingering farewell.

She sat quietly sniffling over Freud's *Mourning and Melancholia* and said her tears were tears of happiness, that she finally understood her urge to destroy, the insight was liberating, she might now be able to disengage herself from the maddening muddle of love and pain. She told me how much happier she felt since Dr. Beuscher had given her permission to hate her mother. The hairs on the back of my neck stood up the moment she uttered the word "hate."

Why did I hold my tongue and not say that I knew intuitively that her analyst's advice was both brainless and life threatening? Why did I not remind her of Graves's *odi atque amo*, the marriage of love and hate? Why did I refrain from playing the knowing mentor—something I normally excel in—and spare her my sermon about the path to wisdom, how essential it is to allow ambiguity within yourself, to harmonize contradictions? Freud was one of our standard references, and I couldn't know for sure how he would have reacted to Dr. Beuscher's remark, but I suspected that giving my wife permission to despise her mother would throw open the floodgates of a devastating self-hate. No daughter loathes her mother without hating herself.

Long afterwards, I discovered that Dr. Beuscher was also a mother and had abandoned the children from her first marriage and renounced her visiting rights to follow her new lover, unencumbered by inconvenient obligations.

Boston was swarming with poets in the late 1950s. We went to readings, became acquainted with major and minor bards, accepted their invitations, welcomed them into our tiny apartment, and, in our spare time, wrestled with our demons. She quit her job at the hospital after two months, concocted a plan to do a PhD, then a master's degree in psychology, but she threw all her schemes overboard once she realized it was just avoidance. She found a different job as a secretary and berated me from time to time because nothing could take my mind off poetry and I just plowed on, undisturbed. After we'd invited Robert Lowell and his wife, Elizabeth Hardwick, around to our place, she decided to sign up for his poetry seminar at Boston University. She went to the lectures every Tuesday night, very much impressed by the tales of Lowell's depression and his time spent in psychiatric clinics, his confessional poetry, and his marriage to a writer. She usually returned home extraordinarily keyed up and just a little tipsy. At the lectures she became acquainted with Anne Sexton—an attractive, flamboyant, chain-smoking poetess who, like her, was the daughter of an ambitious, overprotective mother, and also had firsthand experience of suicide. She told me with a hint of jealousy that Sexton had just been released from an insane asylum following her most recent suicide attempt, that for the first time in her life she'd met a woman who was even angrier than she was, and together they were able to have the most delectable discussions about suicide and the death wish. Although Sexton was four years her senior and the mother of two young children, my wife—as was her wont—believed she'd found a doppelgänger, but eventually, her deep-seated mistrust of women won out over her longing for friendship. When she came home one Tuesday ranting about Sexton's extramarital affair with the poetry editor of a large publishing house, griping that their talks tended to lack erudition, and saying that while she could acknowledge that Sexton's poems were good, she did find them a little lightweight, I knew she was protecting herself from too great an identification. If she couldn't absorb another person fully as an alter ego, she closed herself off, became distant and withdrawn, unreachable behind a facade of husband, health, and happiness.

I had trouble hiding the enormity of my relief when we left Boston to begin a trip across America. The busy city—with its now-fashionable manic-depressive poets, the pretense of history and depth, the phony nature and cultivated congeniality—had turned me to stone. I felt as polluted as the Charles River, and I was frightened that—living on top of each other in that fifth-floor cubbyhole on 9 Willow Street—we were poisoning each other. Thanks to her self-imposed—or decreed—gag order, it wasn't until after her death that I learned the true scope of the anger and pain her analysis had churned up in her. The hate and anguish sparked off the pages of her journal in a scrawl that could barely keep pace with the speed of her fire-breathing soul, the letters tripping over one another with disdain and indignation. The only thing I'd been given during that six-month period was a weekly distillation, sometimes offered in the form of caustic poison, sometimes in the form of tears, a little girl's childish blubbering, exhausted from unraveling the bitter logic of parental love, and hopelessly tangled up in paradoxes. She described with a grimace of revulsion the house she grew up in, its suffocating stench of women, the strong reek of prying, worry, conformity, and self-sacrifice, referring one minute to her mother as the loveless, emasculating murderer of her father, and the next blaming herself for his death. She went on to hate everyone who made her feel guilty and then looked at me like a deer in the headlights, wondering why in God's name she felt guilty about not feeling guilty. Suicide was the perfect means of punishing her mother for a failing love, while in turn complying with the longing to join her father in death. It was all a terrible muddle.

I am convinced that the power of imagination enables us to forge a bond between our darker, sometimes terrifying inner world and the objective, rational world outside us; to unite things that seem divided and opposite—male and female, good and evil, destructive and creative. Throughout the history of mankind, true poets and writers have done little else in their stories and verses than to report on this risky, difficult but healing capacity. We must look our demons in the eye, tame the wolves, hunt down and kill the Minotaur in that labyrinth of our soul, because if we don't, they will destroy us. If my bride, after listening with endless patience, sometimes spat out that she'd had enough of my didactic preaching, I knew I'd overplayed my hand and had over-whelmed her with what I considered the ultimate and sacred task of every writer and poet: using the Word to help others reach the same conclusion. If, at the time, she had repeated to me more often that I wasn't there yet, that there were still wolves howling inside me that I couldn't hear, I might have realized sooner how right she was.

I listened to her wolves and turned a deaf ear to mine. I read her drama and kept my own script firmly shut.

We borrowed Aurelia's car and loaded the boot with everything we'd need for a two-month camping trip in a natural environment neither of us was familiar with. Still anxious about the absence of a pregnancy, she again visited a gynecologist shortly before we left. This one managed to find a physical cause and didn't put the blame on her nerves. She was upset about the diagnosis of an obstruction, felt disgusted by the idea of a clogged body, imagined the most horrific visions of the future, and made our last weeks in Boston a living hell. The prescribed procedure turned out to be simpler than expected and afterwards, according to the doctors, there was nothing standing in the way of conception. On that sunny July day in 1959 when we drove away from 9 Willow Street and set course for the west by way of the north, we had no idea that there were three of us. The gods always hold something back, whether it's fire or the knowledge of good and evil, to force their creatures to dance to their tune.

How much genuinely remains in our recollection of time, of all those years, days, hours, minutes, alone and together, at home or on the road, of the conversations, impressions, arguments, events, encounters? What becomes fixed in our memory and is replayed afterwards in frozen images and crumbling litanies, and why are those particular moments selected from the daily stream to be saved in photographs and filmlike scenes complete with subtitles?

In the history of a marriage between two writers, their texts are the fallout. The rooms we lived in were strewn with our notebooks, manuscripts, typescripts, loose sheets of paper—hers in neat stacks or clipped into binders, mine spread in disarray until she dealt with them. It went without saying that I never opened mail addressed to her or read her journals, and as far as I know, she didn't look through the notebooks in which I recalled events or jotted down ideas for stories and poems, even though—since the incident on the Smith campus—she had become jealous and suspicious. After her death, when, appalled and dismayed, I worked my way through the sentences of her life and the devoted, precise descriptions of people, surroundings, objects—all exercises to force her to observe the outside world, to report on it like a professional writer—I almost drowned in her pain and sorrow, and it's taken me many years to retrieve my own memories, filtering them like sand through the sieve of her creations, to retain my own glittering nuggets of gold—pure, unsullied time.

We drove thousands of miles across a magnificent America and were as happy as could be. Freed from the city and its people, escaped from the confinement of four walls, eyes on the horizon for the first time in ages, we could fill our lungs with air, profoundly impressed by the wide-open rural landscape, a nature whose character changed dramatically every few hundred miles, savage and gentle, enormous and mystical. The mountains, prairies, canyons, deserts, and volcanoes preserve a history which precedes the birth of an immigrant nation, safeguarding the beginning of time—ancient, unspoiled, untouched, and invincible. Its casual recording of millions of years is in strident contrast with the forgetfulness bathing its hasty population, as if history presents some threat everyone is permanently fleeing, and everyone begins a new life—without pedigree or origin—the minute they set foot on Ellis Island, cut off from their roots, without the silt of a family.

We drove through Ontario to the islands of Wisconsin and then on to North Dakota. We pitched the tent somewhere new every night, preferably in a campsite with all the creature comforts, but if need be in some sheltered spot that seemed suitable. She was as astonished and overwhelmed by the beauty and mystery of the country as I was. We often stopped to get out of the car and grab hold of each other, a feeble embrace meant to strengthen us in the face of our insignificance when compared with these majestic wonders. Leaning against me, she said she enjoyed feeling completely irrelevant for a change. The only veil that sometimes obscured her cheerfulness, often at night when pitch darkness descended from one moment to the next, was her growing fear of infertility. The more barren the landscape we drove through, the more frequently she compared herself with scorched earth where nothing grows.

Why do I remember that mouse, scurrying around furiously in an arid, prickly bush in the charred moonscape of the Dakota Badlands? A minor detail, you might say, in light of the eternity in which we wandered like astonished children, but I see us standing there, arms wrapped around each other, near the tent we'd set up—too tired to drive on—on ground forsaken by God and man, burned coal-brown by the merciless sun, the air in the distance blazing with a subterranean smoldering fire, a hellish place where we both felt spied on by invisible enemies. We were startled by a sound rising from a thornbush, an incessant, frenetic clamor from the depths of a spiky torture chamber. A terrified bird, I thought, fluttering in a prison of pain, or two animals, rushing around in that cage of thorns, one chasing the other. But it turned out to be a solitary mouse whom Darwin had lured for incomprehensible reasons—tattered nerves or pure joy—into manically wasting its precious energy.

Memory is literary by nature. It takes factual events and gives them a metaphorical charge, lending what really happened a symbolic weight, persistently in search of the security of a story. For too long I had denied myself access to anything directly autobiographical. At that time I stubbornly maintained my mistrust of the subjective, clung to my teacher T. S. Eliot's adage, and defended the impersonal in poetry as if my life depended upon it—so it was not that summer in the wilderness when I opened the door to what was to be the greatest liberation of my soul. Instead, I find myself opening the door now, as the racket of a lone mouse keeps me awake and I realize that mouse was me. Now, in retrospect, I know my bride had a clearer view, that she immediately incorporated the outside world, made it part of her mythology, furnished it with meaning. In the dark we sat outside our tent and watched a phenomenon we'd never seen before and one I've never seen anywhere since. A dark-blue vapor rose out of the earth and slowly reared up like a gigantic snake which seemed to be watching us. We sat still and whispered, as if this would repel the attack of something monstrous, and I asked her what it was. She replied—as if it were obvious—that this was evil.

You don't easily forget an encounter with a bear. After her death I often dished up the story to the children when they were little, telling them an exciting adventure about their mother and me in Yellowstone Park before bed. Daddy and Mummy, travelling through America like nomads and driving all day long, hot and tired, finally reached Montana. We'd just discovered that Frieda was with us—although we didn't yet know that she was a girl or that she was called Frieda—and were really happy and excited to be having a child, and of course extra careful. In Montana we entered the famous Yellowstone Park, where the bears roamed free, as gentle as lambs eating out of visitors' hands, and babies and toddlers—even smaller than my children—could take a ride on their backs, their hands gripping the big brown bears' thick coats, while the daddies and mummies cheered them on and snapped hundreds of photos. Many of the animals in the park were tame and trained to entertain tourists; even the birds of prey listened to their trainer's voice and flew gracefully on command, then returned neatly in a perfect dive, feet outstretched like landing gear, to the arms of their keeper, who rewarded them with a juicy lump of meat—or a little mouse. Their mother and I came up with a game. We guessed how many bears we'd see in the park—whoever said the correct number would win. She said fifty-nine and I said seventy-one. For five days we travelled through the huge park, from campsite to campsite, counting every bear we saw—two, three, twenty, thirty, fifty, fifty-four, fifty-five, fifty-six, fifty-seven, fifty-eight! Until the very last day, when we'd been driving too long. It was already getting dark, the tank was almost empty, no petrol station in sight. Increasingly anxious and afraid, we looked for a sign to guide us back to our campsite. Staying in a car overnight in the park was strictly forbidden, because at night, outside the light of the cameras, those obedient bears went back to being themselves and became a good deal more dangerous. I could scarcely believe that those benign teddy bears harbored any malice, but I told the children their mother was much more sensible. She could already see the newspapers

reporting on a couple of poets found brutally torn apart in their demol-
ished car in Yellowstone. Using the last drop of petrol, we finally made
it back to our campsite, where campfires kept the bears away all night.
But on that particular evening, the place, normally so peaceful, was in
turmoil. A dreadful agitation prevailed. The campers were screaming
at each other: the bears were coming! People grabbed whatever was at
hand to make as much racket as possible and chase them away: they
beat wooden spoons on pots and pans, tooted their horns, rattled rub-
bish bins, and shrieked at the tops of their voices. Their mummy hid
in the tent, terrified that something would happen to her and Frieda,
while I hastily carried all our food to the car and hid it in the boot.
It was dark, the moon rose, peace seemed to have been restored. We
zipped the sleeping bag up to our noses, although it was still warm. My
small ax was freshly sharpened, ready under my pillow, just in case. In
the middle of the night, I suddenly heard glass clinking, then a ripping
sound near our tent. Their mother and I were wide awake in a flash. I
grabbed the little ax from under the pillow and looked out through the
gauze of the small tent window. What do you think I saw? Not five steps
from us, a life-sized brown bear, the most dangerous of them all, had
pushed in the side window of our car with its strong claws and—supple
and lithe as a circus artist—squeezed its way over the back seat and half-
way into the boot. Growling, he snatched at the bags, sacks, and boxes,
hauled them out, ripped them apart, and ate and drank everything he
found. Oranges, soup, pancake mix, canned peaches, Ovaltine, bread,
eggs, crackers, canned beans, fresh trout, water, milk, fig cookies—and
chocolate. The car shook wildly back and forth, he slurped and smacked
his lips, snuffled, snorted, and chewed, even grabbed the steel ice chest
with his enormous claws, breaking it open like a sardine tin. Quivering,
their mummy and I listened to the sounds, afraid of stirring and drawing attention to ourselves. It went on a very long time. Until dawn.
Suddenly a car drove onto the site. The camp ranger, our salvation! We
held each other tight with relief. (At this point in the story, the children

and I held each other as tight as we could.) We heard the bear thudding away from our car, but where was he going to hide? Behind our tent! Exhausted from his binge, he stood sighing heavily by the tent, just next to their mother's head. Fearing for our lives, we looked at each other. Hardly daring to breathe, we waited until he crept away and complete silence fell, quiet and peaceful.

Mummy had won—that was the fifty-ninth bear.

Children tend to demand the same story over and over again, and with time, I didn't even have to say that last sentence. When Frieda and Nicholas shouted the famous number in unison, they were chanting the formula that meant it was time to sleep. I tucked them in, gave them a kiss, turned out the light, and walked rigid with loneliness out of the bedroom, carrying with me the part of the story I'd left unsaid.

In the morning she returned pale and trembling from the washhouse. She'd heard that that night, before selecting us for his raid, the bear—her bear, the fifty-ninth—had killed a woman on the neighboring campsite with a single, powerful swipe of its paw. Thank God I hadn't done as that woman did, that I'd stayed in the tent instead of storming outside ranting and cursing, wielding a tiny little ax to chase the bear away with my manly bellowing. I could have been killed. She wanted to leave now, at once, as the bear might still strike me down on the spot. I knew her emotions got the better of her and that she drove recklessly when she was angry or afraid, so I took the wheel, leaving behind a scene of devastation, and drove out of the park and out of our exciting story. I glued the clumps of bear fur I found on the back seat into my Shakespeare, but that too failed to survive our scorched Eden.

Two months later I hadn't a clue as to why in her version of the adventure she had me—the character of the husband—killed by the fifty-ninth bear after all. Much later—when an English magazine published "The Fifty-Ninth Bear"—it led to still more indignant attacks by my friends, and especially my sister, on my bride.

"She's free to write what she wants," I defended her. "It's fiction."

"Nothing's fiction with her," my sister replied bitterly.

In Yellowstone, we still had no idea she was pregnant. I'd woven my daughter into the story to extend the meager three years she'd really known her mother by as many days as possible. We suspected it in Pasadena, during a visit to Frieda Plath, her father's sister, whom she'd never met and whom she now devoured with her eyes, in search of family features, of herself. During the sessions with Dr. Beuscher in Boston, she'd given her father's coffin a good rattle, so the omnipotent Otto, now shaken awake, popped up in her dreams and memories with increasing frequency. It didn't surprise me that in those months of analysis, he made his voice heard through the Ouija board, which assigned him royal if not divine status. I don't know who steered the finger that made Prince Otto a mere pawn of a greater power and placed him under the regime of a certain colossus. Childishly excited by her father's visits, she asked question after question, her voice sounding like that of a seven-year-old, timid, awed, and squeaking with the bravura of a little girl hiding her fears.

Everything we shared—our dreams and ideas, our bodies, our work—blinded me to what we did not share. Like my bride, I longed for fusion, thought it a miracle to be so at one with another person; she was as much my female counterpart as I her male. The lesson I'd been confronted with in America was that the primal images fossilized in my bride's psyche—however European her roots—came not only from Faust, the Lorelei, Beethoven, or even nature, but from Superman,

Mickey Mouse, and *Gone with the Wind*; that the marriage of Arthur Miller and Marilyn Monroe had made a deeper impression than the love between Romeo and Juliet. I'd learned that death was less symbolic than I'd thought—sometimes it was the cocoon she would shake off to liberate the butterfly of her poetic self, but just as often it represented a real death, as contemporary and genuine as the fruit of our union which she carried with her in wonder. Later in our pilgrimage, in the Grand Canyon, as we waited for a sign, overwhelmed by the water's language—that fruit was greeted by a perfect drumbeat, *paum!* that still occasionally wakes me with the same goose pimples that rose on my arms thirty-nine years ago.

Unbeknownst to me, the colossus had travelled with us like a stowaway, from Ontario to Montana, and via the Pacific Coast Highway from San Francisco to Los Angeles—he sat next to her when we drove through the Mojave Desert, stared into the depths of the Grand Canyon, watched over our shoulders in New Mexico when the black cloud of bats—guided by an unerring radar—suddenly returned to Carlsbad Caverns, like a bunched-up body recoiling from an oncoming storm, and he travelled with us via New Orleans and Washington to New England, where his wife awaited us. My bride had begged me not to tell Aurelia about the pregnancy, she wanted the child to be just ours for as long as possible. In the car we joked about how we might slip up and unintentionally reveal the secret. Only in retrospect did I learn from the journals that the secrecy wasn't intended to build a romantic bond between us—she was simply terrified that her mother would snatch the baby away like a vampire.

During that time I was putting the final touches on a collection I called *Lupercal,* for which I had immersed myself in the study of fertility rituals. What I was really exploring were the entanglements of any family, between fathers, mothers, sons, and daughters, those knots of love, worry, jealousy, and rivalry, of creation and destruction, with which each of us starts life, threads which literature constantly picks apart to describe the sweet pain of that legacy. I was just twenty-nine and—overcome by a hellish shyness about all things personal—searched for images and metaphors for the wild feasts of indulgence and cannibalism in the world most familiar to me, that of all-powerful Mother Nature. I delved into my memories of England to call up the bestiary I needed to illustrate her urge to nurture and destroy. My bride pointed out that I was gone, no longer roaming America with her, but strolling over the heath of West Yorkshire's Calder Valley.

I was never worried by the fact that my fatherless bride sought a father in me, just as in her I recognized and loved the alertness and clairvoyance of my mother. Nevertheless something had changed in the way she had understandably projected his image onto me, something that at times disturbed me, as I was unsure how to confront it. The conversations with her analyst, the visit to her father's grave, the sessions with the Ouija board resurrected a different Otto from the idealized God the Father to whom she had introduced me in the beginning of our marriage. The erudite, absent but nevertheless loving teacher emerged with increasing frequency as a brutal, jackbooted executioner who made the Nazi salute beside the radio, listening to the sounds of his youth, a voice barking out over the Atlantic Ocean the glorious promise of domination and eradication. In the run-up to fatherhood, I was less than pleased at being identified with an amalgam of God and fascist. What I hid from myself—but the poet brought to the surface in his verses—was the fear of what my bride saw, with her revelatory view of the demonic: my shadow, my doppelgänger, the black soul with whom I wrestled.

Yaddo, an artists' resort in the midst of the woods of Saratoga Springs, New York, is a Victorian mansion surrounded by smaller buildings, comfortably furnished to allow writers, painters, and composers to work in complete peace. It was the beginning of September 1959, but the earthy smell of the woods preserved an eternal autumn. As a married couple we were assigned a large bedroom on the ground floor, complete with bath and walk-in closets, in which she could deposit her predominantly red wardrobe, which would soon cease to fit, and I my meager clothing and fishing tackle. She was deeply convinced that she was pregnant with a son, and we called him Nicholas Farrar, after the only famous forefather I could claim on my mother's side, a courageous, artistic, religious man whom T. S. Eliot immortalized in *Four Quartets*, a literary godfather whom as young parents we were keen to invite to the cradle of our firstborn.

I worked contentedly in a small hut in the woods, and my bride— rejoicing at the space, the large table, and the view of the trees—took the top floor of the house. We soon settled in. Every morning we breakfasted in the mansion with twelve other guests and then went our separate ways—with a packed lunch provided—to a room or hut to work. Never before had we been surrounded by so many like-minded people: solitary men and women who lived for their work, visibly both present and absent, simultaneously outward-facing and introverted, accompanied in spirit by self-created friends and enemies of paper or paint. In the evening we came together in the big house, enjoyed a luxurious dinner, and then sat around the open hearth or attended a lecture by one of the guests. I was having the time of my life, so was distressed a few weeks later to notice my bride increasingly coming to breakfast with greasy hair and a red nose. In the three years of our marriage, even a slight cold had become enough to alarm me, because it could have been the beginning of the sinusitis which had tormented her since childhood, a malady that deprived her first of her senses—she could no longer smell, see, taste, or hear anything—and then robbed her of her sentences. I kept quiet about the strands of hair hanging limp, pasted to her skull, firstly because I didn't care and always found her beautiful and attractive in all her manifestations, and secondly because I knew it was a symptom of depression. She stopped getting out of bed. For a couple of days, every morning and evening I took a tray to the bedroom, where, slumped among the pillows, surrounded by books, manuscripts, loose sheets of paper, and wads of Kleenex, she struggled against her lethargy. Using breathing exercises, hypnosis, massages, I tried to lure her from under the bell jar, to temper the panic attacks. When I asked her what was making her so anxious and gloomy, she gave varied answers. It was too quiet and monastic at Yaddo, she missed the bustle of Boston, hated the sterile white room in which she worked, she couldn't get anything done and considered herself a lazy pig who didn't deserve this luxury, she was sleeping badly and in the couple of hours she did sleep she was plagued by nightmarish images of disfigured babies, dying in childbirth, her mother devouring our child. She couldn't write and on the occasions that she succeeded, she thought every sentence worthless; yet another publisher had rejected her first collection, and she knew herself well enough by now to know that she would hate our son if she didn't succeed in making a name as a writer before his birth.

"Set those old poems aside," I said. "Get your shoulder under something new."

She followed my advice, filed the old poems away, went to sit at the Hermes, and, behold, a miracle occurred. Just before her twenty-seventh birthday, she typed ceaselessly, for hours on end, possessed, inaccessible, biting her swollen lower lip, a feverish blush on her cheeks, the scar of her previous death standing out crimson with excitement. She wrote one poem after another, and I saw, heard, and read how she gave birth to a different voice on paper, a new sound, the previously unheard heartbeat of the poet she had so persistently and tirelessly sought. Even the streams of sound with which she rolled out the poems in the evenings—excited but controlled—had changed, undulated with greater warmth and wrath, suffering and satire than I had ever heard before. Astounded, I saw before me in the most magnificent strophes and stanzas the creaking, aching trees of Yaddo, the pears like fat little Buddhas, the dead moles like blind twins, the all-consuming matriarch of mouths, the dead father like a fragmented colossus whom she had to glue together in her hours married to shadow, the town where they mend men and shoot volt upon volt through her brain. And I remember that—after reading out one poem from the "Poem for a Birthday"—she walked over to me, her belly revealing the gentle, self-confident curve of that other creation, and in surprise bent over to stroke my face. Tears were sliding unnoticed from my eyes.

"How did I do this to you?" she asked.

"You'll be as good as new," I recited.

I was convinced that there, in Yaddo, I was witnessing the birth of her poetic self, that for the first time I was hearing the voice of the raging, wounded woman she was, whom she had buried under adaptability, superficiality, cheerfulness, and ecstasy, a woman who one day needed to reveal herself if she didn't want to self-destruct. It was the clearing of the throat—still patently influenced by a number of confessional poets—that paved the way for the poems she left behind for me more than three years later on a cold Monday morning, the day she exchanged her body for the Word.

I have no idea what happened to the painting, I'm not even sure we ever owned it, but I wish I could get my hands on it now, to study in detail what Howard Rogovin saw when he painted her portrait. The morning sickness was gone, she felt stronger, read and wrote, went back to eating with her old voracious appetite, became beautiful in a way I'd never seen before, and proudly agreed when Howard asked her to pose for him. Curious as to the slow emergence of my bride's double in paint, I asked to sit in while he worked. The friendly, talkative American didn't see any problem, and so the three of us ended up in his light conservatory: model, painter, and poet. The pine cones crackled in the wood burner, outside the rain played on the conifer branches; she sat upright on a stool wearing a Mona Lisa smile—impossible to gauge whether it was mocking, contemptuous, or wise—and I looked back and forth between her and the portrait in the making. I don't know when it happened, how many sessions I gazed at her alongside the painter who danced before the three-legged easel as if entranced, when suddenly Howard became alarmingly agitated and, adding a dark color to his palette, hastily sketched an apelike assailant behind my unsuspecting bride. He'd told us that when concentrating deeply on a painting, he often heard voices or saw unknown creatures that struck him as sufficiently real to be immortalized directly on canvas, convinced that they were summoned up by the model and heralded something he sometimes only understood years later. I saw from her raised eyebrows that she'd read a fearful premonition in my face, and she looked at me, questioning, worried. I looked on, motionless, as everything in me demanded I take action, jump up, and protect my pregnant wife—prey to an unknown danger—from the sinister shadow figure behind her. Just then a small snake meandered over the dusty studio floor, stopped, and raised its head. I called out to the painter, distracted him from the canvas, told him to look at that magnificent, hypnotic creature on the floor.

"You like it because it's evil," said Howard casually.

Our stay at Yaddo ended after eleven weeks and we returned to Wellesley, where we arrived just in time to celebrate Thanksgiving with the family. Our departure put an end to the creative reverie in which she'd written a poem a day, twenty-one in all, the best ever, a collection she christened *The Colossus*. To her they represented the justification of motherhood.

Aurelia saw in the blink of an eye that her daughter was pregnant. In order to play out the secret charade to its conclusion, we visited a doctor for official confirmation. Our son—who at his birth turned out to be a daughter—was five months old. For the time being, he bore the name we would only really bestow on him twenty-six months later, and in an ominous poem, his mother burdened him with a weighty heritage of suicides and harsh stars—the specters of her own fears. He was on the point of making his first big journey, to the country where he would be born as a she. Once again we packed our possessions into boxes, suitcases, bags, and sacks, stored them until our departure in the tomb of her first death, and went on a three-day trip to say goodbye to friends and family. On the day of our departure, Aurelia brought us to the station in Boston. Huddled in a thick winter coat, her features contorted with concern, concealed indignation, and desolation, she stood on the platform, and we waved until she disappeared from sight. In a burst of pity, I even called out to her that we'd come back to America in two years' time. No one knew that my bride would never see her fatherland again.

Once again she eased the pain of her departure by denigrating that which she had to leave and fanatically singing the praises of the England to which we were returning. The moors, the literary life, London, even the weather, beat America hands down. The constant stream of rejections in response to her first collection, a couple of stories, and a children's book, and missing out on prizes and grants, had made her increasingly mistrustful. She saw exclusive networks and cliques everywhere trading favors and prizes, regardless of the work's quality. She'd once had a brief affair with an editor at a prominent publishing house and was convinced that the horned god was blocking her and rejecting from on high everything she sent him, filled with self-indulgent resentment. In exile she could begin with a blank slate, freed from a web of self-pollinators and bootlickers, and she would again have the soothing buffer of an ocean between herself and her mother. The analysis had made her realize that she saw all editors, publishers, juries, committees, critics—the entire outside world, in fact—as fragmented representatives of Aurelia, with the same power to give or withhold love. She could win her mother's love only by being successful, and since this cold exchange filled her with rage and hatred, she thwarted Aurelia by being unable to put pen to paper.

We were forced to abandon our plans to live in Rome for a while and travel through Europe, and instead searched for a house where our first child could be born. Money worries resurfaced. We stored our things temporarily with my parents at the Beacon. Thanks to my friend Daniel Huws, we were able to stay in London with him, his wife, Helga, and their young daughter at a familiar address, 18 Rugby Street. We took a room on the second floor, slept in a sagging single bed—which my friend said would seriously test any marriage—shared the only WC to grace the house, in the damp basement, and from 18 Rugby Street we were able to begin the exhausting, depressing search for affordable accommodation in London. Before we embarked on that task, we celebrated Christmas at the Beacon with my parents and my sister, who had come over from Paris.

Everyone around me thought me overprotective of my bride, saw her as possessive, demanding, and jealous, and me as an obedient dog, a sleepwalking bridegroom who couldn't see how manipulated, drilled, and trained he was becoming. They forgot that everything she saw and felt, I underwent as if I saw and felt it myself. Her pain was my pain, her fears were my fears, except I reacted differently. In retrospect, after her death, I asked myself in the blackest moments whether she might have been more resilient if I'd been less patient about the tantrums, punitive sulking, cold-shouldering, if I'd been more rebellious, made fewer adjustments. As long as we were together, unseen, sheltered from the inspectors prying into our relationship, I loved her without judgment. It was the hostile gaze of others that made me loyal to her without hesitation. I regularly felt like a man protecting a fox from his own barking hounds while the fox bit him. We didn't talk about it, but when she said on the way to Heptonstall that she was so looking forward to seeing my sister again, I knew she wanted to please me. In reality she was dreading it.

The minute you enter your parents' home, you're right back in your familiar childhood script. The family division of roles remains unchanged, the cues are ready; the festering subterranean tensions, secrets, and unspoken accusations flare up, proving their inextinguishable might. Although I walked in as a father-to-be, with a radiant pregnant wife at my side, both of us on the threshold of a new role, my father and mother's welcome, their glances, the smell of the coal burner, the light in the room, the rain on the windowpanes, the sound of the screeching wind around the house, all brought me back to the archetype of the youngest son, of the sibling who missed his older brother and found in his sister his first female mentor and confidante. For two years I'd wandered a different continent, freed from the burden of oppressive silence from a father traumatized by World War I, from being the child who listened to nocturnal cries of fear from a man calling for his mother on the battlefield, but once home I heard them again, reverted to the mummy's boy, too ashamed to ask his father about Gallipoli, the only child who'd stayed near the valley, who had never abandoned his mother but still fell miserably short because he could not possibly replace the prodigal son.

My sister arrived the day before Christmas. My bride and I waited for her in the doorway of the warm living room, and—like a seismograph attuned to the vibrations of her nerves—I felt her tension. Olwyn's appearance on that cold December day can justly be called ravishing. Unruffled by the journey, in a stylish suit, with a new, modern hairdo, she embraced me at length before turning to her sister-in-law, tactlessly forgoing any form of greeting, and crying out in surprise, "What happened to your hair?" My bride automatically reached for her tresses, no longer dyed blond, checked herself, stiffened, and shot my sister a cold look. I touched her neck, felt the tendons—suddenly thickened and contracted—preparing her for flight, gave her a squeeze, and told my sister we were expecting a baby. Back in our bedroom my bride cried with homesickness. She yearned for central heating, a Christmas tree with glistening baubles, and her mother.

We sat in a drab pub by the canal in Hebden Bridge, pressed together, our mood as dark as the blackened walls, her fruit juice stale and musty, my Guinness cheerlessly cold. Our hunt for a house in rainy and windy London had been futile and left us exhausted. We had wandered the city for days, climbed narrow stairways, visited one flat after another, and returned dejectedly to Yorkshire. The apartments we liked turned out to be too expensive or didn't accept children; the cheap places were grimy and dilapidated. Our first child was due at the end of March, and we were gradually coming to feel like Mary and Joseph in search of a room at the inn. As I sat there, my arm around a despondently sobbing wife, I could suddenly picture a house, a crystal-clear vision of the place where we were to live. Carefully I explained to her what I envisaged, near here, a dirt-cheap paradise, surrounded by an immense garden where she could grow roses, keep a vegetable patch, an orchard where we could pluck the apples from the trees. I described it in detail as if I already owned it: the drive leading up to it, the security of a cobbled courtyard, the fields of daffodils, a nearby river where I could catch fresh fish each day. I didn't mention that I could see two distinct houses, that beside that paradise there was a horizontal and a vertical stone, surrounded by the low wall of a graveyard. I didn't know who the vision was intended for, and I'd kept quiet about the palpitations and the chest cramps that accompanied it.

She wouldn't consider living in the countryside, close to my family, far from the theaters, libraries, publishers, and parks of London. Once we'd spent a couple of days regrouping at my parents' house, we took a train to resume our search in the city. This time we had some help from friends we'd met in Boston, Bill and Dido Merwin, who'd moved to London before us and proved to be guides and guardian angels. It was January 1960 and within a week, thanks to them, we found a cramped, affordable flat at 3 Chalcot Square. The Merwins lived around the corner, knew everyone who was anyone on the literary circuit, were warm and helpful, and offered us the furniture and utensils they had in their attic as well as the use of Bill's study when they were in France. The house was being renovated, but we could move into the empty flat on February 1, giving us two months to prepare for the birth. The *London Magazine* bought two of her poems, Heinemann had agreed to publish *The Colossus*, *Lupercal* was released by Faber & Faber and received glowing reviews, my first collection won a prize. Bill worked regularly for the BBC and put me in touch with the makers of the Third Programme, the best of radio broadcasting on the subject of culture. We were on the threshold of a new life, as poets, mother and father, and truly thought our demons had turned into angels, our vampires into nurturers.

We painted, sanded, and varnished. I lugged the boxes upstairs, built a bookcase, painted the kitchen and the narrow corridor vermillion at my bride's request, shoved the Merwins' furniture back and forth until everything fitted, and put a small card table under the coat rack opposite the front door so I would have my own work space. We ignored our guardian angels' advice to buy a secondhand bed, oven, and fridge—my bride was horrified by the idea—and bought them brand new, fulfilling a promise I'd made to her when we decided to return to England. In the sitting room we hung the two lithographs our friend Leonard Baskin had given us, had the image of Isis enlarged and framed, and, with her portrait, finished furnishing the apartment. Thanks to the prize, the jubilant reviews for *Lupercal*, and the radio programs on the BBC, invitations flowed in for interviews, publications, lectures, presentations, and dinners—enticements from the world which made me uneasy but to which my wife replied with conscientious enthusiasm. Living in London, near Regent's Park, the zoo, and a Tube station, meant lots of coming and going. Friends I hadn't seen in years dropped by, drank, smoked, sang, and enjoyed the lunches or dinners my bride tirelessly continued to serve up. In the meantime she'd grown as round as a cannonball so that she could barely turn around in the tiny kitchen, and when I helped prepare a dish, I couldn't get past her, no matter how I tried. Initially she remained the good-humored, radiant hostess, fulfilling the dream of a house full of arguing, laughing, singing, and drinking intellectuals, but as the pregnancy wore on, she was quicker to tire and soon became moody. A month before her due date—sick from the smoky living room, the bustle, and lack of rest—she begged me to put an end to the daily stream of visitors, so I regularly turned people away at the front door with the excuse that my wife was sleeping. It went without saying that we made an exception for a good friend like Lucas Myers, on his way to America, or my sister, who brought a companion over from Paris for a weekend.

My bride never knew that Chalcot Square was where we opened the door to the people who betrayed our love, our life together, my remaining life. I've seen the scenes in our house—her aggressive silence and jealous possessiveness, my pathetic meekness—described by people who were close to me or by passersby I had nothing to do with. I once confessed to a friend, half grinning, to having counted how often she'd called my name that morning while I worked in the narrow corridor—104 times—and even that had ended up in the gossip mill.

After her death, friends and foes, acquaintances and strangers, descended on us like parasites, feeding on our blood, making a travesty of who my wife really was, with their narrow-minded, restrictive view, sometimes even working on the sickening assumption that they were supporting me with their hateful memories of her. I read the eyewitness accounts of our marriage with horror, and, to me, every revelation of my private life felt like a flogging. And I remained silent.

Frieda Rebecca was born in the unfurling morning of Friday, April 1, with her Prussian grandfather's light-blue eyes, her mother's facial features, and the Hugheses' dark hair. In the months preceding the birth, I'd taught my wife breathing exercises and hypnosis in an attempt to eliminate her fears of an un-American, natural home birth—something Aurelia dreaded. I implanted the idea that it would happen quickly and seamlessly, promised not to leave her for a second, to whisper mantras to her, to lure our child out with melodious singing. Aided by an Indian midwife, my bride gave birth to her first child with unimaginable strength and surrender, gave birth to herself as a mother and to me as a father, lay at the center of creation, radiant with the anointed child in her arms, baptized by her blood and our tears. And the death we'd brought with us in our knapsack, the stowaway on all our journeys, seemed to have been rendered innocuous, deceived by life. The only thing I couldn't prevent—powerless magician—was our daughter being born on the day of fools, something my bride had feared, lest the frivolity of a joke should forever cling to the child. It didn't seem to matter when—pain numbed by happiness—she stumbled to the telephone to call her mother and tell her, crying, that she had brought *ein Wunderkind* into the world.

He stood at the door holding his young son's hand, which gave him an innocent air and prompted me to drop my guard. At that time, Al Alvarez was the most influential poetry critic in England, the kingmaker among editors, who had turned the *Observer* into the make-or-break newspaper for poets. He was my age, a short, compact man, his face wreathed by a thin beard, and he probed me with two different eyes, one open and curious, the other half-closed and mistrustful. I liked him instantly. He'd asked for an interview, and we'd arranged to do it while walking with our children. He waited in the living room, where my wife was dressing Frieda, while I sorted out the pram downstairs. That meant I missed the conversation that she reported to me when I got back, blushing with shame and regret. She had called herself Mrs. Hughes, but had assumed that Alvarez knew who she really was, and thanked him for selecting the poem he'd published in the newspaper a year previously. The critic had looked at her uncertainly, clearly having no idea what she was talking about. It was as if she'd had to explain the punch line of a joke, she said, when she described the poem she was talking about. He realized who she was and, surprised and apologizing, said her maiden name. She'd howled in misery once she'd heard the front door fall shut behind us, feeling she'd made a fool of herself in front of the most important man in the British literary kingdom. I reassured her, described how kind and intelligent Alvarez was, how pleasant the conversation had been, how he'd openheartedly spoken of his struggles with depression, that he remembered her poem well, thought it different from anything that had landed on his desk from America, and that we had nothing to fear from him. How was I to know that this very apostle of poetry would play a leading role in the posthumous worship surrounding my bride, would become the catalyst of a cult in which I was assigned the role of traitor, the murderer of a saint? As so often happens, Oscar Wilde was right when he said that all great minds acquired disciples, but it's always Judas who writes the biography.

We took turns caring for our daughter so that my bride had several hours each day to rest, read, and write. The first weeks after the birth, she wandered through paradise, blissfully happy, goddesslike, and glorious, touched by something so great she had the illusion of being invincible, beyond reach of the evil spirits who turned her into a crying child or—from one moment to the next—into a fury, the terrifying male growl welling up from a cavern of her throat, the voice first heard over the Ouija board, when Pan had seemed to speak through her. I thought the protective halo of motherhood would never disappear, that the birth of a child would shield her forever from the whirlpool of death, that she'd been given a pardon for a sin she'd never committed—a murder she hadn't perpetrated—but from the moment she announced that she wanted to write, that for too long no sentences had occurred to her, as she longed for the poet, the old demons stirred again, the tormentors, whispering that she was worthless until she'd realized her dream of success, dragged her back into the turbulent inferno of fear.

Meanwhile my fame spread like a vine, tied me up like a snake in its greedy tentacles, elusive, mysterious; an uncontrollable, unprunable process of parasitism and appropriation. It was out of my hands, and I didn't realize right away how it was slowly suffocating me. The more prominent I became in the world, the more I came across images and descriptions of myself in newspapers and magazines, the more threatened I felt, prey exposed to the knowing gaze of strangers, who acquired a remote power over me. People had already made up their minds about me before I met them, which obstructed any form of normal contact. The conflict for which my stars had destined me at birth became heartrending. Leo—lit by the sun, overexposed, applauded by everyone, admired and scrutinized—fought against the ascendant of Cancer, which cherishes nothing as much as its security, invisibility, and secrecy.

It was the end of April and I was wandering through London, thirty years old, praised and honored, fragile due to a frightening happiness and the wakeful nights with a crying baby, the unaccustomed father of a child who was ignorant of the weighty task she had to fulfill on this earth. I was perplexed by a nostalgic longing for the person I had once been—or thought I'd been—when in the middle of the bridge, I came across a young man carrying something hidden away under his jacket. I froze in my tracks in disbelief at what I'd seen and looked into the pleading, coal-black eyes of an orphaned fox cub, and a helplessness swept me back into the endlessness of my childhood. It was as if there on that bridge I stood opposite myself, opposite the boy who had freed a small red-haired fox from a trap, picked him up, bundled him under his coat to keep him warm—dizzy with his clingy, familiar closeness—and was taking him home to his mother's house. He was mine for a pound, I heard the young man say. In the couple of seconds that I hesitated, I saw myself coming home to the cramped apartment on Chalcot Square and, instead of gold, frankincense, and myrrh, laying a stinking fox at my wife's feet. I walked on. Something or someone inside me told me that with every step away from the starving fox, I was walking further from myself, and from us.

She dragged me along, pushing the cooing baby in the pram, and repeated excitedly that I'd be as surprised as she'd been, it was a sign, I'd see. A couple of minutes' walk from our house, we turned the corner of a street I often passed through on the way to Primrose Hill or Regent's Park, as it was where Yeats had lived, and in doing so I felt I was paying homage to the poet who had accompanied me every day with his poetry. She stopped outside number 41, cheeks flushed with incredulity, and pointed to a sign at the window: **For Sale**. She knew there was no way we could afford it, but all the same, this was the house she wanted to live in with me, and look, on the first floor I'd have a room to myself, where I could work undisturbed. And on the top floor there were at least four small rooms, enough for all our children's beds, at the back there was sure to be a room where she could put a desk so she wouldn't disturb anyone as she rattled away at the typewriter. Here in Fitzroy Road, lured by the spirit of Mr. and Mrs. Yeats, was our home for eternity, one we would never have to leave, where we would raise our expanding dynasty, entertain friends, grow old together. She said of course it was a dream, but what seemed impossible now could become a reality in the future. And I said that, just to be sure, I would call the agent to ask the price, you never knew. We walked on to number 23, stopped at the steps leading to the front door, and looked at the blue plaque that like a great seal verified the existence of "William Butler Yeats 1865–1939 Irish poet and dramatist." There we were, my vibrant wife filled with dreams of a time to come, our beautiful daughter in a pram, and I remember that—staring at the last words, "lived here"—I was overcome by a sorrow as heavy as lead. I thought it was sadness at transience and death, the unsettling thought that I'd given a child life that one day would end, and that our lives too would be things of the past, hers and mine, poets who might one day have a blue plaque in London with the inscription "lived here." I didn't know we were standing outside the house where, eighteen months later, on a cold Monday morning in February 1963, my wife would put her head in the oven and turn on the gas.

There was a market for stage and radio plays; reading them aloud for the BBC paid well, and—with the underlying idea that a successful play would secure sufficient income for an entire year—I threw myself into it. In retrospect it's lucky that most of what I wrote then was lost, and that we used the backs of the typed-up drafts as scrap paper or—like so much else—misplaced them when we moved house. Loyal to poetry and Shakespeare, I opted to write a drama in verse, something I'd discussed during my first visit to T. S. Eliot and which he'd encouraged. Fascinated by the mythical theme of the fragmented self, I wrote a play about it, laden with metaphor, with a lamentable dearth of real characters, strong dialogue, and dramatic development, an esoteric creation in which I felt I was illuminating the torn modern Western identity, failing to realize that it was about me—about us.

The amazing thing is that only Aurelia, who kindly attended a reading of the play in Cambridge, Massachusetts, hit the mark when she explained to me in an intelligent, critical letter that the level of abstraction went over her head. Supported by my bride, who thought it unbearable that her mother should make a single negative comment about my work, I vigorously defended it, but Aurelia was right, *The House of Aries* was a failure.

My wife was ecstatic at the publication of her first poetry collection, a couple of days after her twenty-eighth birthday, and went into a slump of equal proportions in subsequent weeks. At the newsstands we bought the important newspapers and magazines on the days when the literature reviews appeared, leafed through them in anxious anticipation, and disappointedly cast them aside each week because there was no fanfare about *The Colossus* anywhere.

Every writer cherishes the fantasy of a debut that takes heaven by storm, of headlines with exclamation marks, articles in which literature's professional gatekeepers immediately recognize the creator's genius, enthusiastically announcing the discovery of a new voice. The longer the wait for these headlines, and the more it looked like the debut had been ignored, the greater her insecurity. She began to doubt her talent, expressed regret at including old poems in the collection, stillborn children as she called them, immature fetuses in formaldehyde, rhetorical, academic artifacts, monstrously unreal and contrived, imitations of a few heroes from her pantheon but then talentless and riddled with worms—something everyone could now see with their own eyes, something that would make her the laughingstock of literary England, and after that public humiliation, how could she face all those literary greats at all those get-togethers and cocktail parties now that she was nothing more than the little American wife of the award-winning English poet who also desperately wanted to see her verse in print? It didn't matter that I said that it could be months before a poetry collection was dealt with, that novels received priority in reviews, because of course poetry appeals to the eternal and is therefore more patient, in less of a hurry than contemporary prose, which often—sadly—allows itself to be hastened by the breath of current affairs and fails to reveal the everlasting.

In mid-December I set off with the proud mother and humiliated poetess to spend Christmas at the Beacon, my own little family in my wake. Although she never said it in so many words, she missed the chain mail of public praise to protect her from perceived condescension on the part of my sister, who—she believed—obstinately refused to acknowledge her as my wife. The memory of a number of painful incidents during the previous Christmas, and of the spiteful confrontation with Olwyn at Chalcot Square—which they entered into in oppressive silence by stubbornly taking turns to open and close the window of the smoky sitting room—had set their relationship on edge. I was at a loss as to how to deal with this growing antagonism. The only thing I knew for certain was the hurt and anxiety with which my wife reacted to the slightest hint of disloyalty. This was also the reason that, after some pleading, I caved in and granted her request to invite not Olwyn but Dido Merwin to be Frieda's godmother.

Salvation came from Al Alvarez. Four days before my sister arrived at the Beacon, his enlightening, glowing review of *The Colossus* appeared in the *Observer*. I bought a bottle of champagne to celebrate, placed an extra copy of the newspaper in my sister's bedroom, and hoped that the recognition by the god of literary criticism was sufficient to shepherd us unharmed through the weeks in Yorkshire. Olwyn arrived on Christmas Eve, showed no sign of feeling wronged that we had passed her over as godmother, admired our nine-month-old daughter with as much exuberance as her inherited reserve allowed, congratulated her sister-in-law warmly on Alvarez's review, listened willingly to her somewhat overexcited report of an exhibition she'd visited, and seemed to be thoroughly prepared to avoid friction. In self-defense I ignored the unnaturally peaceful behavior of the two women, angels who tiptoed through the room and carefully avoided a collision. That was yet to come.

We had decided to celebrate New Year's Eve at the Beacon and return to London in the first week of January 1961. Nothing much unpleasant had happened beyond a crestfallen expression from my mother when I turned down the BBC's request for a television appearance as poet of the year. A few days before New Year's Eve, I was upstairs in our bedroom writing a new play and a libretto. At Yaddo I'd met a Chinese composer working on an oratorio based on *The Tibetan Book of the Dead*. Under a parasol of pine trees, we'd talked for hours about rites of passage, and—laughing and flushed with enthusiasm—he'd introduced me to the Eastern take on the universal quest. When he asked me to adapt the book for a libretto, I didn't hesitate, but immediately set to work and had since made a daily task of examining the soul's longing for purity.

Outside, a falling snow transformed the Calder Valley into a postcard, the voices of my family rose gently from downstairs. Only when something in the pitch of the murmur changed did I become alarmed. What until now had sounded like the rippling of a brook became a swirling current in which Olwyn's voice rose to the top. I walked downstairs, found my wife in the doorway of the sitting room, arms crossed in front of her like a barricade, her slender neck rigid with rage, and wearing a stony look that made it clear to me that something had gone badly wrong. The moment she seized hold of me and—spitting with indignation—hissed into my ear that my sister had just sneeringly called her Miss Plath, Olwyn burst into a furious tirade; accused her sister-in-law of rudeness, intolerance, egotism, insensitivity; said she was behaving in her *own* parents' house as if *her* word was law, that she took no one else into account, kept her brother locked up out of some sort of sick jealousy, hadn't even offered her a place to sleep in Chalcot Square the previous March, insulted her friend from Paris by ignoring her completely, and that with a belligerent, aggressive silence she made sure that everyone in the house trod on eggshells so as not to disturb her own refined spirit. It wasn't until she paused that Olwyn seemed to realize she had Frieda on her lap. My wife—who'd frostily allowed the accusations to wash over her—detached herself from me, walked toward my sister, snatched up our child, turned, and stomped up the stairs.

We left the following morning before dawn, placating my parents with the excuse—not entirely untrue—that their daughter-in-law was bothered by a nagging stomachache. Woken by the clattering, Olwyn was up in time only to wish us a pleasant journey from the top of the stairs. My wife didn't react.

It was the last time they saw each other.

In the first weeks of the new year, her fury raged like a fire under her skin, occasionally transformed into a fit of impotent crying and the occasional mumbled curse, in which she called my sister an envious bitch or shriveled witch. Jealousy was the only satisfactory explanation we could come up with for the outburst. To make it clear where my loyalty lay, I said that Olwyn had once had literary aspirations but that she'd soon realized she would never become an original writer. In my wife's eyes, the source of Olwyn's jealousy wasn't the publication of her poetry collection, it was me, her almost incestuous love for me. Olwyn would never tolerate another woman at her brother's side, certainly not now that my love for her was perpetuated in glorious motherhood; that the withered, passionless loins of servile secretaries like Olwyn and Dido could never bear authentic let alone creative fruit, because they didn't know what it was to be a woman, because they secretly felt equal to the men whose trousers they wore and labored under the comfortable illusion that their paymaster's talent and intelligence were really their own.

She calmed down only when a doctor's examination made clear that she was pregnant with our second child. He'd also advised her to have her appendix removed, a simple procedure, he told her, but the prospect of an operation gave her nightmares about hospitals, knives, amputations, bleeding to death. For me the arrival of a second child brought money worries. I was looking for a way of earning enough to support my growing family without having to look for a regular job that would eat up my sacred time. Since a writer could earn more at the BBC than anywhere else, I had the idea of developing a program for children, offering them a structure for extending, ordering, and understanding their experiences through poetry. The more I thought about it, the more enthusiastic I became. The class of boys I'd once taught came to mind, and the effect that reading poems had had on them, the way they slowly let down their guard and something in those closed faces opened up to the music of language, the swell of rhythm—they wrote their first poems, which were often moving in their simplicity and directness. The thought that many of them might now be working on a production line, and were equipped to counter the monotonous droning of the machine in their head with the melodious phrases of "The Waste Land," made me so happy that I couldn't wait to pitch my plans to one of the producers.

A part-time job came up for my wife like the answer to a prayer. Editing texts for a booksellers' advertising catalogue distracted her from the fear of hospital admission. She edited from one until six while I looked after Frieda. I had to force myself not to spend all of those hours watching the little gnome, sitting beside her on the floor and cunningly coaxing the babble that so fascinated me: a small animal with the gift of language. Thanks to the libretto, a new play, and the outline of a series of radio programs to work on, however, I could usually resist the temptation. It rained, it was misty, and I remember the talcum-powder-scented happiness of those hours with my daughter. I also remember being unable to trace the cause of a disquiet and a nervous anxiety that flared up occasionally. There seemed to be no reason for it. My bride's debut collection had now been reviewed here and there in favorable terms, we attended readings and presentations, met Theodore Roethke, one of her literary idols—critics often accused her of imitating him—and we gave our first joint interview for the radio program *Two of a Kind*, in which I described our unique, telepathic bond as one of Siamese twins, so strong that it was as if we were part of a single spirit.

Was it one of my countless defense mechanisms to protect her and myself against those who looked down on our marriage? Was my proclamation of loyalty during a broadcast an attempt to reach my sister? Or was I trying to make up for a remark earlier in the interview, the tragicomic simultaneity of our answer when the presenter asked whether our marriage was one of polar opposites, and I said we were considerably different just as my wife pronounced us more or less the same?

If I committed hubris in proclaiming to the world that I could read her thoughts—at any moment in the day could feel what she felt, knew her through and through—then the gods have punished me severely for my arrogance.

The look she gave me when she handed me the receiver should have been warning enough, but I was too full of my own plans, ignored the piercing eyes of war, and agreed to meet the female producer in half an hour near the BBC building.

"Sultry voice," my wife remarked, but again I ignored the signs, explained simplemindedly that the producer was Irish, that all Irish accents instilled in me a homesickness for a country I didn't come from; I kissed my wife and daughter, promised to be home around lunchtime, and closed the door on an unscathed 3 Chalcot Square, to find it, on my return two hours later, in complete havoc.

The producer had been enthusiastic about my proposal, offered some suggestions on which I made notes, assured me that the BBC would agree to it and that I would be able to provide at least three broadcasts. It was getting on for one o'clock when I hurried home, proud of the successful negotiation and the prospect of receiving a substantial fee that would keep the wolf from the door until the end of the year. As I climbed the steps, I looked forward to being able to draw my wife momentarily out of the mire of gloom, so I could not have been more astounded by what I found.

In order to open the apartment door, we had to push aside the card table I worked on in the hallway. I was surprised to find that the door wouldn't budge, that she'd mistakenly put the table back—quite unlike her. I called her name, heard no reaction, forced my way inside, and stepped onto a carpet of shredded paper bearing the erratic motif of my handwriting. The table where I had left my notebooks, a pile of poems, and the play was empty. It was difficult to tell whether the vermillion haze before my eyes had taken on the color of the walls, or whether it was my blood, pumped to the roots of my hair by a rampaging heart. Like Theseus, I followed the path of torn paper leading to the sitting room, where my wife awaited me like a Minotaur turned to stone, nostrils flaring with a snorting rage, surrounded by the bible-paper pulp of my copy of Shakespeare, which was similarly torn to shreds. The vengefulness I'd so often seen flicker in her eyes had changed into an unmoving, opaque black, a gaze with which she silenced me. She put on a coat, grabbed her bag from the sofa, snarled that she'd be late for work, and disappeared without another word.

A couple of days later she lost the child that had been due on August 17, the day I was to celebrate my thirty-first birthday.

Pain, regret, and shame tethered her to her bed and swept away the haze that had stirred the hysterical fear of abandonment, the mistrust and jealousy between us. She couldn't bring herself to apologize for the destruction of my work and my favorite book, and I felt unable to raise the subject, hamstrung by my understanding, sympathy, and dismay. Pale and slumped among the pillows, she grieved for the lost son or daughter, was all the more glad of Frieda's lively closeness, and worked feverishly on a number of poems, as if she had to compensate for the loss of a child by bearing as much poetry as possible. When I later read in one of her letters home that she'd promised Aurelia she'd make her a new baby as soon as she could—and I didn't know whether to roar with misery or rage—I understood in whose eyes she'd failed the most. At the end of February, she was admitted to hospital for the appendectomy. She was called up rather unexpectedly, we couldn't find a babysitter in time, so I stayed home with Frieda and only went to see her that evening. With her thick hair in a plait, her fringe anxiously combed over the scar, wearing a high-necked white nightgown, she was preparing, scared and serene, for the death and resurrection her mythology predicted. No one but my bride would have made such a drama of an appendectomy. I visited her every day, brought food from home because she disliked the bland hospital meals, and I saw how my restless, lively spouse—who normally couldn't sit still, always animated and fidgeting—grew to enjoy the horizontal, passive state in which she was excused from daily life. Every one of the poems she'd entrusted to me in case she didn't survive the procedure was an allusion to birth and rebirth, interspersed with an unconcealed disdain for childless women such as my sister and Dido Merwin. Her subsequent poetry about her stay in hospital was what first made me realize her longing for death was not just the siren call of a dead father for whom she had to sacrifice her life, but was also a much more banal, regressive longing for a life without husband and child, without cares and responsibilities, and without the pressure to become famous.

She suffered sleepless nights because she missed her mother, wrote exuberant letters swearing that she couldn't wait until June when she would come to London, see our daughter for the first time, and they could spend entire days together, yet Aurelia had not been at Chalcot Square for a day before her mood darkened. Her love for her mother flourished best on paper, at a distance. As soon as she felt Aurelia's eyes upon her, she transformed into a faltering creature who looked at herself through her mother's gaze, where she constantly fell short. In order to surprise her, she had saved up the news that she was pregnant so that she could share her joy directly with her mother, but Aurelia's first reaction was to frown deeply with concern and ask whether her daughter was sufficiently recovered from the miscarriage—she had to restrain herself to avoid shooting an accusatory look at me—and only when she saw my bride's disappointed face did she force a smile and congratulate us.

We set off in our new Morris Traveller, on our way to the coast to make the crossing to the Continent. Aurelia stood with Frieda in the doorway of Chalcot Square and waved us off encouragingly. Once out of her mother's sight, she began to weep softly with relief and the unfamiliarity of two whole weeks' separation from her child, entrusting her to the care of someone else. She had started on a novel during her mornings at the Merwins' studio. She would say nothing more about it than that it was about her first death and that it was good for the book to have her mother around, because now she remembered in greater detail her childhood irritations, strain, tension, and fear of failure, called to mind by her nitpicky, judgmental presence.

Before we drove to the south of France to join the Merwins in Lot, we spent a few days on the coast. Only when I lay next to her on the pebble beach in the sun, listening to the crying seagulls and the convivial rejoinders of the surf, did I notice how the past months—or years—had exhausted me. For one who saw himself as imperturbable, the involuntary clenching of my muscles, the subcutaneous trembling of my nerves, and the restless, clearly palpable beating of my heart were disconcerting, as if someone else had possessed me and was trying to take control from the inside out. At night I dreamt wild, anxious dreams of collapsing houses, unable to find the way out, buried under rubble. When interpreting dreams, I've found that the house is generally a symbol for the self, and its demolition indicates a transitional phase in personal development, so I read the stars to see whether they supported such a sharp transition.

It was increasingly difficult to remember who I was.

The birth of a child had transformed me from the youngest son into a father, and the increasing fame made me so visible that I didn't know how to fulfill my need for anonymity. The prize for my first collection had to be spent abroad; being compelled to travel made me rebellious, as if I had to pay for the privilege by handing over control to the outside world. My second collection had also won a prize, my wife's debut had been published in America, the BBC asked us to collaborate on poetry programs more and more frequently and also commissioned me to write new works for the radio. The literary world now struck me as a hungry predator that would devour me from top to toe if I did not wrest myself from its claws in time.

It was there on Berck-Plage that I suggested to my wife that we go and live in the countryside. I confessed how desperate I was for trees, air, earth, water, for birds and fish, for peace, the two of us working together, each in our own room, focused, without the temptations of the metropolis, away from the tentacles of public life. I added our shared fear of the atomic bomb to the mix, pointed out that in the countryside we would be outside the fallout zone should a bomb ever be dropped on London. In her eyes—so familiar to me—I saw the struggle between resistance and assent, between irritation and compassion. I saw the thoughts flit back and forth, the attachment to fashionable living and the desire to do right by me, to do what was right for us; saw how she calculated the balance at lightning speed, the pros and cons of country life, a place where she would have me completely to herself but would have to forgo the pleasures of the city. When we returned to our hotel that evening, rosy from the sun and the salty sea air, she had agreed. We would look for a house in Devon or Cornwall.

I still wonder if that was the biggest mistake I made in our marriage.

The following morning we set course for the city which in retrospect I wish we'd never visited, although my wife particularly wished to see the cathedral with her own eyes.

The name Reims still sends shivers down my spine.

We found a small hotel near the overwhelming edifice, stood before it, entered, and, in the ensuing hours, understood why the Cathedral of Notre-Dame was built the way it was: we felt like insignificant worms, controlled by all that was more powerful than ourselves, transient playthings with no free will, at the mercy of the eternal and sacred.

It happened the following morning, when we were sitting on a terrace in the shadow of the Gothic bulwark, each with a bowl of steaming café au lait, a hunk of baguette, and a croissant. My wife had bought a pile of postcards depicting the cathedral and—frantic and devoted as a schoolgirl—was writing on the backs, charting an impression she could process only once she'd found the words. I looked at her that chilly morning, her mac fastened, hunched over the serrated prints, biting her lip, and I thought about what I saw, the magical duplication of genuine and photographed surroundings, the experienced and the described world, the dauntless attempt to hold fast to that which is transient, under the watchful eye of an indestructible monument to the great departed.

I was startled out of my reverie when suddenly, from nowhere, a dark, stocky figure appeared next to her, a Gypsy woman shrouded in colorful rags with a leathery face, wrinkled and bony, every line etched with a sharp nail. Proudly, and with a routine show of pride, she held up her wares before my wife, two medals on a pendant, a Saint Nicholas and a Mary. Without glancing up to look danger in the eye, my wife turned her down with a resolute *non*. The bolt of lightning in the Gypsy's eyes was something I recognized only from my own wife, a deadly stare, intended to turn the enemy to stone or rubble. My wife wrote on stolidly, so she didn't see what happened, how the Gypsy pointed a purply-black finger like a gun barrel at her right temple and shot a curse like a bullet: *"Vous crèverez bientôt."* You will soon be dead. As she darted away, supple as a weasel, my heart contracted, and I—superstitious servant of the goddess of the thousand names—wanted to run after her, buy up all her wares to lift the curse. But I sat there as if paralyzed, held down by the lead weight of a foreshadowed death, and did nothing. For days the words of the Gypsy echoed in my head, tolling like alarm bells, and I prayed that the jinx was not valid if the damned hadn't heard it herself, that the walls of the crypt where my bride hid to write were strong enough to protect her against all the evil in the world.

Weary from the hours of driving, in the evening we arrived in Lacan de Loubressac. The Merwins awaited us under a sparkling starry sky, with a richly laden table, at which there sat a beautiful dark-haired woman, a

Spanish duchess it later emerged, who—to my bride's consternation—was also staying at the none-too-large house. Since I'd read the poems in which she sarcastically ridiculed our generous guardian angel—not just as one of her reviled infertile women: she'd also openly referred to Dido's face-lift—I had to repress the grating shame of knowing about a betrayal soon to take place. I would have been less troubled by guilt had I known that I would one day become entangled in a web of revelations, that everyone we'd ever met, with whom we'd eaten, drunk, and laughed, would crawl like rats from a reeking sewer to present themselves as the evangelists of a drama they'd witnessed, and in their epistles mete out judgments in comparison to which my wife's poetic stabs shrank to pinpricks.

The summer of 1961 was the last time the Merwins saw her. The prelude to our cutting short our five Gallic days in Lot was set in motion the evening we arrived. Bill Merwin had described the limestone plateau on which the village bordered in lyrical terms, a godforsaken landscape, unnaturally flat with unexpected protrusions, unsightly little rocks that looked as if they had been kneaded by an easily bored child and abandoned unfinished. Since my bride announced that she wanted to do nothing but lie in the sun, our host suggested he visit the plateau with me the following morning. Her reaction was unexpectedly sharp: she claimed to have been planning to explore the area with me first thing the next morning. Without any fuss, I agreed and promised to go walking together, suspecting that she was afraid of being left alone in a house she didn't yet know, that she felt uncomfortable about the extra guest and the secret of the new pregnancy, something she didn't want to tell the Merwins just yet, fearing that it might go wrong again. The openly disdainful look Dido shot at her husband escaped no one, but I was used to this sort of reaction and had no wish to condone my wife's behavior. The evening wore on, it grew too cold to sit outside, and we moved to the sitting room. To lighten the mood, Dido put on Handel's *Messiah*, and, with the erudition, liveliness, and dastardly humor typical of the English aristocracy, name-dropped about conductors, sopranos, and tenors who had passed through her childhood home, talked about Job, the Psalms, Proust, as always peppering her account with French and Latin, and proved herself a full-fledged connoisseur of music by pointing out allegros, fortissimos, and moderatos. While music meant a great deal to me and my work, to my tone-deaf wife it was more impenetrable than fine art, and she was confused rather than comforted or uplifted by this show of veneration. In the middle of the chorus about sheep gone astray, she stood up, announced that she was tired and wanted to go to bed, and lingered waiting for me until I said that I would stay up to listen to the music a while longer. Half an hour later we heard stumbling on the stairs, she flitted through the room in a fluttering nightgown, and without a word rushed outside, into the night. Of course I immediately rose from my seat to go in search of her.

Twenty-eight years after our visit, I read Dido's personal outpourings about our brief stay with the Merwins in one of the countless biographies. Her memoir formed an appendix to the book Anne Stevenson wrote about my wife's life, and by extension our life. By then I had read one mendacious biography after another, seen my wife's martyrdom grow to iconic proportions, and found myself accused in these hagiographies of being the murderer of a genius. Knowing that after her suicide the world needed a scapegoat and that nothing I said about my life with her would be believed, I did not react to a single accusation, refused to cooperate on biographies, gave no interviews, remained silent. Stevenson was the first biographer to receive my sister's approval. Olwyn managed the literary estate with me and saw it as her primary task to protect me like a hellhound from the sensationalist, intrusive outside world. My sister's approval meant that from that moment on, the accusations took on a more dangerous form and I was again torn between my loyalty to two women.

To be honest, I laughed initially at Dido's malicious memories and was perplexed at the unabashed outpouring of venom. Our aristocratic friend—who in my wife's published letters had seen herself described as the very thrice-married wife of a famous poet, fifteen years her junior, who later lost even her third husband—wrote as she spoke, witty, clever, liberally peppering her tale with phrases such as *ipso facto*, *petit bourgeois*, *embarras de richesse*, *casus belli*, showcasing her ready knowledge of world literature in misogynistic, Strindbergian scenes featuring my bride, who paralyzed those around her by deploying a judgmental silence like nerve gas, maintained the appearance of an ideal marriage like a B-film actress, punished a husband the minute he paid attention to other women, used up all the warm water, and raided the entire fridge to satisfy her Pantagruelian appetite. I thought it inevitable that Dido's characterization of my bride as a "vessel of wrath" would boomerang back at the writer herself, and that it would be clear as day to every reader that she was dipping her pen in the same poison. Although Dido understood as little about the love between my wife and me as all the other soulless eyewitnesses, the tigers of revenge are often wiser than the trained dogs. I cannot deny that I was relieved to finally read a description of reality, even if it was exaggerated by the writer and completely missed the mark.

Of course I was also aware that the panic attacks, silent treatment, and fits of crying—however seriously I took the wound from which they sprang—were mind games, but I had become too attached to the breathtaking idea of being so important to her that she couldn't do without me for a second. Raised by a mother whose heart went out to those absent more than those present, for whom I was the substitute for the prodigal son, I was unshakably addicted to my bride's desire for my palpable proximity. Her capacity to play every muscle in my body, to interpret every look, and even to follow me in my dreams was part of an intimacy I had never before experienced, and marriage made clear to me how much I had longed for it. I ascribed my unreliable heart, the feeling of being suffocated, the nervous tics and nightmares to the commotion, the alienating power of fame, and the distressing lack of nature.

What Dido or any other accuser of our marriage could not possibly know is how in the night from which I plucked her—shivering in a nightgown, drowning out her fear of abandonment by swearing about the ridiculous profusion of falling stars—we were connected by a bizarre dream, how in the morning, surprised, we compared the images that had visited us in sleep: a coffin and a cathedral. I had anxiously kept quiet about the Gypsy's curse, but was not surprised that its ominous power had sought an outlet and in my subconscious had found itself stuffed into a coffin. Remarkably enough, neither of us dreamt of Reims Cathedral but of Chartres, the blackened, thrice-resurrected temple, with its pagan labyrinth underfoot, a building I knew only from books, but which she had visited on her own before we were married. Familiar with the cryptic disguises of truth in a dream, I thought it was primarily about the meaning of the word *chartres*, which was meant to tell us that we had to chart or map out something together. But what? The way I remember it, the images of our dreams merged, although I know for certain that in mine she smashed a jug and gave the shards to her mother, and in hers, she received a letter from her father, delivered to our home in the coffin. The message was short and clear: Daddy was back and he wanted to come and stay with us.

It took us a few days to drive to the coast, and on July 14 we crossed the North Sea on the last ferry to get back to our daughter, anxious as to what she'd learned while we were away. She was already able to say "Dada"—a word which she unfortunately considered applicable to every man—but since we had not yet succeeded in eliciting a "Mama," my wife was afraid that our little clown would have been so brainwashed that she would now say "Granny," while she herself as mother would remain nameless, having to make do with an angelic look, bursting into joy whenever she set eyes on her. Besides missing Frieda, she was also itching to continue with the novel she had by now dubbed *The Bell Jar* and consistently dismissed as a potboiler, a women's novel intended to fill the coffers, bread-and-butter writing like all her prose. She could already picture the description in a publisher's catalogue, joked that the word "heartrending" would certainly appear, preferably accompanied by the characterization of the heroine as "tragic" and "talented" and the drama as a "mental breakdown." She thought the phrase "suicide attempt" would be bad for sales, although of course that was what it was about.

"The book's writing itself," she said. "I don't have to make anything up."

When I cautiously inquired as to the other characters, she confessed that a good many people would easily recognize themselves and that she had given them plenty of reason to feel horribly betrayed. She knew for certain that her mother, former lovers, friends, and benefactresses would be hurt by her merciless portrayals, which was why she had decided to publish the novel under a pen name.

"Victoria Lucas," she said triumphantly. "Light prevails."

"Or Lucifer wins," I said.

Aurelia, convinced of the importance of the word "Mama," had practiced during the holiday with Frieda—continually holding up a framed photo of my wife—until the desired recognition was effortlessly regurgitated, and for days she had been pointing at the portrait and joyfully trying out the new word. She was therefore confused when we returned to Chalcot Square and she saw my wife in the flesh, probably thought that the word referred only to the image and couldn't understand why her grandmother kept asking, "And who's that?" Before she hesitantly pronounced "Mama," she turned her head from the original to the photo on the shelf, her success reinforced by a little round of applause from Aurelia, who with this undoubtedly well-meant welcome gift had underestimated my wife's fears and jealousy. I saw her stoically hold up the mask of cheerfulness and gratitude, but I knew that it would slip off at night and I would find myself lying next to a sad woman who, faced with her daughter's confusion, felt robbed of one of the most important firsts in her child's life.

After we had spent a week with Aurelia and Frieda visiting my parents in Heptonstall, my wife and I went in search of a house in the country. My mother-in-law wasn't planning to go home until the beginning of August, so she took care of our daughter, who was clearly fond of her. It was only later, when she was a grown woman and poet, that she would distance herself from her grandmother by refusing the love of a copy, not allowing herself to be cherished as the replacement for a dead daughter.

We wanted to live within four or five hours of London, and the agent sent us a list of eight houses to visit. We were both impressed by a somewhat dilapidated, ancient but picturesque farmhouse, a former vicarage near a church with a graveyard, in the north of Devon; two floors, twelve rooms, a cottage, a stable, a walled and cobbled courtyard; surrounded by a substantial stretch of land with an orchard. It was the house I'd seen twice in my dreams, once after our return to England and a few nights before our search began, a haunting dream in which the place capsized and out of the central well slithered a gigantic golden serpent.

"This is Eden," said my bride.

We bought Court Green in North Tawton, Devonshire, with financial help from both our mothers, without knowing it was not destined to be her house for eternity but mine. We rented the apartment on Chalcot Square to a married couple with whom we felt an immediate connection, a Canadian poet and his wife. He, like all poets, was introverted and shy; she a dark-haired beauty, daughter of a Russian Jew and a German Protestant, with hips that seemed designed to bear countless children. But she proved to be a specimen of the category my wife sneeringly dubbed very thrice-married, childless spouses of men of stature.

No paradise without a snake.

The meeting with Assia Wevill was to change our lives forever.

I found the plot again after my wife's death, when I read the letters that were in Aurelia's possession. First I had to get over the shock that she had given even the most intimate love letters—the ones I had written in 1956 full of yearning desire, when we were newlyweds keeping our marriage a secret—to her mother for safekeeping. The second shock came when I read a letter in which I rediscovered myself as the lovesick shaman who—convinced of his own abilities and generous with his abundance of ideas—helps his secret bride devise stories by bombarding her with dozens of possible plots. One of the story lines I offered her was about a married couple who flee the city and withdraw to the countryside. They use their disappointment with urban life and longing for peace and solitude as a pretext, but their real motive is jealousy. They dream above all of possessing one another completely and are weighed down by the tacit fear that their passion will be threatened by the temptations of a provocative social life. For a while they are extraordinarily happy in their large farmhouse, but over time they miss their friends. They increasingly invite people to stay with them, and in the seclusion of the house, their contact with visitors takes on a more intense flavor than was possible in the city. She begins to fantasize about her husband's affairs with their female visitors, he worries about her around the men in the house. Their country idyll falls into disarray. They have opened the door to the danger that they had intended to escape, and the marriage is seriously threatened. In my proposal they stop receiving guests, look for a smaller house near the city, and their union weathers the storm.

Reality had a different epilogue in store for us.

It sounds uncanny, but I have seen my suspicion proven right too often to be able to ignore it: whenever I work on prose—come up with a plot, write a story or essay—what I write becomes a terrifyingly accurate prediction of an incident that will one day take place, as if writing it calls the event to life. The grimmest manifestation of this was yet to come on the day I ran over a hare on the A30 between North Tawton and London. After that, it was years before I wrote prose again, in fear of this phenomenon. It's not hard to guess why I've spent the past five years immersed in Shakespeare, unraveling him in an extensive study—blind and deaf to the scorched fox telling me to stop. I understand what a writer means when he says that the book on which he is working will be the death of him.

On August 31, 1961, we drove in a fully loaded Morris Traveller to our new life in Devon, stopped in the main street of North Tawton to quickly buy a pan so we could warm up some milk for Frieda the minute we arrived, and got there before the movers had been able to fill the house with our things. It was raining, a thick fog hung over the countryside. I remember that my heart skipped a beat with love when we crossed the threshold and my pregnant wife smiled bravely and told me how much she enjoyed the sound of raindrops on the thatched roof. We were here because of me, because I was fleeing a world that threatened to cripple me and rob me of everything dear to me. And she'd followed me, full of faith, with the same courage with which she fought her demons on a daily basis and a willingness to make the best of life at Court Green. I had not yet realized that the life I was running away from was not only the stifling enticements of London but also my life with her, that I had ended up—slowly and without noticing—under her bell jar, cut off from myself, gasping for air. All attempts to liberate her from the scenario of an inner tragedy, to break the shell in which she was locked, against which the real life she longed for was constantly deflected and remained out of reach, seemed fruitless. The voice that briefly rose in the birthday poems, to celebrate the birth of a new poetic self, had not been completely silenced on our return to England but had simply grown fainter. Shortly before we moved to Devon—seething because I was home late—she'd wielded the high stool to smash my mother's heirloom mahogany table to smithereens. I preferred her rage to her crippling despair, so I stood like a boxing coach outside the ring and cheered her on: That's it, go on, smash it to pieces, give it everything you're afraid to put into your poems! Only when she'd calmed down and my racing heart had returned to a slower rhythm did I soften my words. That poet was inside her, I said, I'd heard her, in Yaddo.

We sleepwalked into the land of Tristan and Isolde. I took the attic, she a large room one floor down at the back. Fixing up and decorating the house and renovating the grounds around it took all my energy and attention, so I soon forgot my haunting forebodings. I took care of Frieda in the mornings so my wife could work undisturbed. In the afternoon I withdrew into the apex of the house, still close enough to my loved ones to enjoy the muted sounds coming from the kitchen or garden. We harvested fruit from the trees and bushes, forked up a forgotten supply of potatoes, sowed and planted, and in the early months enjoyed the idea of living entirely from the land, needing nothing and no one to be wealthy and happy. I made a desk for my wife from a six-foot plank of elm, planed and sanded it until it gleamed like a mirror, and as I worked, I suppressed with all my might the recurring thought that I was polishing the lid of the coffin from our dream.

Meanwhile one of my worries had been pleasantly dealt with. We recounted our dreams to one another each morning, to the extent that we were able to grab them by the tail, although my wife often had little to report because she woke recalling only a sense of fear or a few gloomy images. We'd been living at Court Green for a couple of months when one morning I greeted her with congratulations. That night in my dream, she had won a prize for a story.

I brought her a mug of Nescafé with warm milk, as I did every morning, so she could immediately get to work, and I went back downstairs to light the stove and prepare Frieda's breakfast. Around one o'clock she joined us, as always with a furrow between her brows. The post was delivered during lunch. She leafed through the modest pile and looked at me in disbelief when she recognized the name of one of the countless foundations and committees she tirelessly bombarded with requests for grants and subsidies. She ripped open the envelope and read aloud that her application for the Saxton Grant had been approved, giving her a year to work on a novel. She pounced on me like an agile cat, called me a prophet, and wisely decided then and there not to tell the committee she already had a novel ready to go. The grant of two thousand dollars was to be transferred in four installments, after each submission of part of the manuscript. She would divide up *The Bell Jar* so as to earn money from it each quarter without the pressure of a deadline. I shared her joy and concealed my relief that the novel's publication would be delayed by a year. I dreaded what it would do to her and those around her, despite the cover of a pen name. No matter how much difficulty I had with Aurelia's patronizing concern and grasping self-sacrifice, I didn't think any mother deserved to see herself so heartlessly portrayed in a book.

In the meantime, life at Court Green maintained the appearance of happiness. My now-voluminous bride—who laughingly called herself a fat cow—enjoyed decorating the countless rooms, painting little flowers and hearts on chairs, cabinets, doors, and window frames, laying a red carpet on the floor of her room, using her Singer sewing machine to make red curtains for the sitting room windows, displaying the copper pans on the shelves I'd built in the kitchen, and bravely attempted to withstand the dreaded cold of an approaching winter. The days shortened, the darkness lengthened. When we looked out of the bedroom window early one morning, we saw a full moon spying on us from behind a yew tree while generously casting a blue-white glow over the church tower and the gravestones. My bride had complained that she was stuck looking for a subject for a poem, so I suggested she concentrate on the face of the moon and the yew in front of her, let the image do the work and see what her subconscious made of it. Later that afternoon, wearing the expression of an obedient schoolgirl who'd completed an assignment, she handed me a poem. When I looked up after reading it, I saw from her scowl that she'd been anxiously observing me, curious as to my reaction and at the same time afraid of what I'd found. I read precisely what she'd wanted both to hide and to reveal: a deep sorrow, an inescapable despair, a woman in free fall, unstoppable, who couldn't be restrained by anything or anyone, as always on her way to her dead father. My heart stirred, and I felt myself dragged down by a black melancholy. I'd lost my bride to the seventeen-year-old girl who wrote in her journal that she wanted to be God. She saw how much the poem depressed me. She said with as much self-possession as she could muster that it was nothing, just an exercise.

"No," I said, "it's a good poem, unfortunately."

Our son—who this time we'd long imagined to be a daughter—was born just before midnight on January 17, 1962, swept out on a wave of amniotic fluid. We'd decided on his name, Nicholas Farrar, two years before his birth, and our decision was as fixed as the Saturn-ruled star sign under which he was born. Our little billy goat had to use all his might to batter his way into the world against the membranes of his first shell. His tiny head was crumpled up into a surly grimace, which lent him a surprisingly mature and combative air. Having expected a girl, I looked with astonishment and some dismay at this angry boxer, as my wife described him. I had such a profound bond with my daughter that I was overcome with fear of failure at raising a son. In the early morning I went outside to bury the placenta under an elm, hacked open the frozen ground with a spade, and slid it from the ovenproof bowl into the small hole. I knew I was burying more beneath the earth than just the afterbirth, but I didn't know what it would mean to my wife to now have a son in a manger, in addition to a God the Father and a husband.

"I'm never eating hare from that bowl again," she said when I returned to the delivery room, from which she'd watched the interment, radiantly happy, the child swaddled in a blanket in her arms.

Since we'd moved to Court Green, I was happiest when I woke up around four or five, snuck out, and obeyed a growing longing for invisibility. Just as when I was a boy and had slipped off with my brother in the middle of the night, away from the anguish of our parents' house, watched the sun come up over the Yorkshire heaths, tasted the pleasure of solitude, so too I slipped out of the marital bed, crawled out from under the bell jar, from the claustrophobic embrace of our love, to spend a couple of hours alone, unseen and free. I resumed the double life I'd known from childhood, fled the family to go fishing and hunting, and after a couple of hours returned home with trout from the Taw, a pheasant, rabbit, or hare. I cleaned the catch while she was upstairs working. I gutted the fish, plucked the bird, skinned the rabbit or hare. My mother had taught me to marinate a hare in its own blood mixed with claret, dab it dry, season it, sear it, and cook it slowly in the oven in the crimson marinade. I would never again use the ovenproof bowl spoiled by our son's afterbirth, and refrained from shooting hares for a time, but I did give the animal a role in the radio play I was working on for the BBC, which would contain the most ill-fated prediction I've ever penned.

The Chymical Wedding of Christian Rosenkreutz is one of countless variations on the quest for purity, and I read it while working on the libretto for *The Tibetan Book of the Dead*. The hero's search formed the inspiration for the radio play I was writing, titled *Difficulties of a Bridegroom*. Spurred on by a previous play's rejection and the justly critical remarks of a radio editor, I stubbornly clung to the theme of the torn self following a path riddled with trials and initiations in order to become whole and real. This time, however, I tried to flesh it out with lively dialogues that didn't suffer from esoteric intellectualism. I attempted to turn the bridegroom script into a fairy-tale scherzo, into which I'd worked some outlandish dream images. The poet penetrated deeper into my stony soul than did the confused spouse. He fished out the image of a man-eating tiger from my subconscious, a predator to whom the bridegroom is married off by a bloodthirsty society. Only after withstanding a number of tests does the tiger transform into a beautiful woman. In one of the scenes I was working on after the birth of our son, a hare suddenly crops up and is deliberately run over by the main character while he is on his way to the supernatural woman he secretly desires, who disguises herself as his real bride. I'd never run over a hare or any other animal whatsoever and saw the event in the radio play as a symbolic way of killing the real woman, the original bride, who had to be sacrificed to liberate the other woman from her shell. The bridegroom picks up the murdered hare, sells it to a poacher in town for five shillings, and buys two roses with the blood money, which he then gives to his lover. This scene was played out in remarkable detail a few months later, although I didn't run over the hare deliberately but by accident on the A30, and bought not two but four roses, two of which I smashed and the remaining two I gave to my queen of the night. The decision to go to her that day changed my life for good.

After my bride's death, I came across the hare and the two roses in one of her final poems, like hieroglyphs of my descent. *Difficulties of a Bridegroom* was broadcast on January 21, 1963. She must have listened to it in the sitting room of 23 Fitzroy Road, pale and lonely, shivering with cold and misery, and probably seething with biblical rage at her adulterous bridegroom and the man-eating Lilith who had severed him from her.

Anyone who has lost someone to death knows the pain of hindsight, counting down the final days and hours, marking the months and seasons with a black cross, the survivors' almost unbearable realization that that particular Monday, May, spring, Christmas was a loved one's last.

And they didn't know it themselves. No one knew it.

Every April I see the daffodils re-emerge from the earth around Court Green, indifferent to the lot of man, blind and irrepressibly obeying the drive to make their way from the dark underworld to the light to dance like elegant ballerinas in the wind. And every year I think of her final April, how she greeted this golden-yellow gift of lavish beauty for the first time with cries of awe—and never again. Urged on by our grocer, who told us that all the previous residents of this house had harvested the daffodils and sold them to him, we went to work, cut the flowers with scissors, turning a deaf ear to the plaintively shrieking stems, bundled them in dozens, and brought our wares to the purchaser. The sale of the flowers, alongside the game I shot, the fish I caught, the fruit and vegetables we plucked, reinforced our sense that we inhabited a self-sufficient paradise in which we could live off the land and our work. A visitor took a photo of my bride and our children on Easter Sunday, a holy family stretched out among the daffodils, perfectly illuminated in bold spring sunshine. The scissors—a wedding present—were lost that April, disappeared into the sod, preserving the memory of her small hands like a cross of rust.

I still have the picture. It captured a life of which the children have no memory. I can look at it a hundred times, but nothing in her radiant, innocent face betrays her daily struggle at the elm-wood desk, the attraction of her other self which after the birth of a son claimed the right to exist, made her presence felt, fearsomely growling in every poem that gushed from her more fluently than ever; the threatening, murderous voice of a real self which, no longer numbed by the anesthesia of fanaticism and self-deception, rose up like a snake and hissed at that one absent soul, the God the Father, the voice of Ariel, who would give her a worldwide fame she would never know.

On Good Friday she came down to the kitchen, where I was feeding my daughter a bowl of porridge. Wearing a mysterious grin and without saying a word, she placed a poem in front of me, picked Nicholas up from the carry-cot, and took him outside. After I'd put Frieda down for her afternoon nap, I read "Elm," and I remember my skin crawled and my hair stood on end. I read the poem over and over, as if I could change its meaning by rereading it, could calm the storm it unleashed, temper the roar, but there was no changing what she'd written, and I read it as a portent of farewell. She'd liberated her poetic self, was stuck in the rut of her past shortcomings and carrying out a solitary battle with death.

Daddy was back, and he was here to stay.

From now on the voice of a resurrected self would be endlessly blaming, moaning, and keening. It would coax her into the labyrinth and lure her toward its core, where her father was waiting patiently. The age-old plot, that macabre travesty of a passion play, had finally caught up with us. I was standing in the wings looking on, an actor in the midst of a script that had been ripped to shreds.

Prior to the Wevills' visit, I'd reassured myself with rational explanations that my bride was worn out from the nocturnal awakenings, the breast-feeding, the nappies, the workmen carrying out the final repairs on the house at the crack of dawn. On top of that, she was again plagued by her perennial winter malady and lay feverish in bed taking penicillin to combat her sinusitis. Once recovered, she remained tired and ill-tempered, tried to hide it from me and the children, and poured all her chagrin into jealous attacks on a neighbor, a sixteen-year-old blossom who often dropped in with questions about homework, poetry, or music, hungry for knowledge and attention, and who, after a number of visits, was driven from my side by some catty remarks and a radioactive glare from my wife. Friends from London came to stay during the weekends. We put them up in the guest room and enjoyed discussions that were finally about something other than children, vegetables, and the weather. That spring, our property burst forth with flowering trees and shrubs, white and pink blossoms, a hedge of lilacs, canopies of laburnum, a symphony of colors and fragrances, all set to a chorus of birdsong. Frieda had grown into a proud tour guide and showed the guests around while holding on to my wife's hand. Even though she was exhausted from cooking and hosting a two-day visit and heaved a sigh of relief when everyone left on Sunday, those guests had brought us some of the intellectual life we both sorely missed.

Before we left for Devon, we'd spent two evenings in London with David and Assia Wevill, one at our place and one at theirs. In retrospect it's incomprehensible that my suspicious spouse—who, even without her powers of clairvoyance, saw every woman as a Jezebel capable of luring her husband away—did not seem threatened by this exotic queen of the night, with her jangling golden bracelets, her seductive, flirtatious glance, painted fingernails, silk garments, and that dark, husky voice whose gutturals contained an irresistible hint of German. Assia Esther Gutmann was everything my wife had dreamt of: Jewish, hunted, glamorous, and cosmopolitan.

"She wears her passport on her face," she said with admiration.

From the start, the two women were fascinated with each other, as if they'd met their shadow selves, one from the new world, the other from the old, both in exile. I knew my wife had secret fantasies of being Jewish, heir to a hidden lineage, something Aurelia vehemently denied. Both their ambitious *Muttis* seemed to have been of like minds when it came to methods of child-rearing, and they trumped each other with uncanny similarities, reminisced fondly about typical German dishes, gossiped about shared acquaintances, and squealed with delight whenever they discovered another favorite artist or cherished novel in common. After dinner at the Wevills', we went home with a present Assia had fetched for my wife from the bedroom, a souvenir from Burma, where she and her third husband had been married. As we walked back to Chalcot Square, my wife clutched the carved, hand-painted wooden snake contentedly to her breast.

On the afternoon of Friday, May 18, 1962, I drove to Exeter to pick up David and Assia from the station. Most of our guests were exhausted and chilled to the bone when they finally stepped onto the platform after that four-hour train journey, but this handsome couple exhibited no trace of their ordeal. They came toward me, arms linked and laughing, with slightly more baggage than you might expect for a weekend. Somehow it was evident that they'd spent the entire journey talking, that they weren't just a married couple but good friends, and—as in every friendship—there was a clear division of roles so that her extravagant ways gave him, shy and silent, something to hide behind.

It was twilight when we arrived at our house. I can still see my wife standing in the doorway—Nicholas in her arms, Frieda leaning against her leg—beaming in anticipation, well aware of the image she was presenting to the guests, a mother with two children, a wife and poet, framed within the opulence of a kingdom. The round table in the sitting room—the one the Wevills had loaned us because Chalcot Square was too cramped to accommodate it—was laid with the best china and the house smelled of freshly plucked flowers from the garden, a pot roast that had been simmering on the range for hours, and the aroma rising from the gingerbread just out of the oven.

After our guests had freshened up and Assia had descended the staircase like a film star—a setting sun in an orange silk gown, painted and hung with clanging amulets like a warrior going into battle—we gathered around the table, ate and drank, talked about poetry and mutual friends, laughed about gossip and anecdotes. He was timid, intelligent, and unforthcoming, she was witty, frank, and outspoken, posh and—ten years his senior—devoted like a sister to this fragile Adonis. With the characteristic patience of a spouse hearing his wife's tales for the umpteenth time, he gazed adoringly at the effect she had on us when—self-possessed and dramatic—she recounted the family's exodus from Berlin in 1933, how Hitler almost got his hands on them, how she could still hear the Nazis' jackboots marching past while she hid in a baggage car; her parents, she, and her sister caged like hunted game in various refugee camps before they finally escaped to Palestine via Italy. Around eleven my wife got up, said with some pride that in a couple of hours her ravenous son would wake her, and went upstairs. After fifteen minutes she called me, but I stayed where I was, nailed to the spot by the glance of a pair of gray-green eyes—the irises wreathed by a dark halo—and imprisoned in a cloud of cigarette smoke and Dior, an aroma that overpowered the fragrance of lilacs.

I lay awake for hours in the agonizing knowledge that she was sleeping under the same thatched roof, just six feet away, her boyish husband nestled against her voluptuous curves, her blue-black hair spread like a fan over the pillow, and with the throbbing pain of desire, I imagined the sighs and groans I'd draw from her if I dragged her from that bed and took her. Beside me, my wife descended in her dreams to her father's crypt, roamed hospital corridors in search of him, only to arrive, lost and afraid, at mounds of bloody amputated limbs stacked like firewood ready to be shoved into the oven, whose blazing heat she could feel. The minute she woke, gasping, and clung to me like a fearful child, I tried to calm her with my hypnotist's voice and sketched pastoral scenes to transport her back to sleep without executioners, corpses, and concentration camps. I was still awake when Nicholas began to cry. I grabbed him from the crib, brought him to my wife, and escaped for a couple of hours to the banks of the Taw to calm my nerves.

She was the last to come downstairs, fresh as a morning breeze, smelling like shampoo and perfume, ostensibly dressed for a day out, in a snug cashmere twinset that wouldn't have been out of place at a festive occasion. My wife had set the breakfast table and surprised our guests with a still-warm apple pie, baked in the early hours. While we were passing around the jug of cream, Assia said that last night she'd dreamt she'd been visited by a giant pike. She could see only one eye, a golden globe containing a human fetus whose heart was visibly beating. My wife held the jug in midair, like a freeze-frame, struck by a dreamscape she knew came straight out of my poetic iconography. To hide her mild jealousy, she praised me a little too excessively as a dream-diviner, easily the equal of Joseph from the Bible. I let the moment pass, with the excuse that it had been a late night and my wits weren't sharp enough for a prognostication. I waited before picking up a cup or fork, in case my hands were trembling too much.

Our guest was in love with me, but she didn't know it yet.

I was in love with her, and I knew it.

That morning, in a state of euphoria, I started my descent—deaf, dumb, and blind with happiness.

Enchanted—hunter and prey in one—I knew I would pursue her at any cost. The desire and happiness of the solitary mornings on the Taw, of wandering over the heaths of Devon, ears pricked to the sound of a gnawing rabbit or a fleeing hare, now possessed me all the hours of the day. For the first time in ages, I felt alive, awake, connected to reality and the source of my poetry, so I knew I had to dare to leap into the unknown, no matter the consequences.

I remember little of that Saturday we spent at Court Green. She helped my wife in the garden or lay on a blanket in the sun beside Nicholas, absently stroking his downy hair. I drove her husband—with Frieda on his lap—around the area, ran out of petrol, and gratefully accepted a lift from an army jeep that brought all three of us back home. In the evening we listened to recordings of Robert Lowell, a voice that took my wife and me back to our time in Boston, a cue for my queen of the night to tell us about her first suicide attempt, and to give her boyish husband a chance to criticize confessional poetry in praise of mine.

We sat at breakfast on Sunday morning, after another restless night of passionate yearning. We'd agreed to take the Wevills to the station in Exeter after lunch. Our guest offered to make a potato salad, one of her *Mutti*'s renowned recipes. Confused and aroused, I had withdrawn to the orchard to pick some apples and had come in through the back door and found her in the kitchen, half leaning against the counter, her somewhat plump fingers with their long painted nails grasping a paring knife and a turnip. I could hear my wife talking with her husband in the sitting room.

I stood beside her, pressed as close as possible to the welcome curve of her hip.

"You know what's going on," I said.

She nodded. Just as I was about to plant a kiss on her neck, my wife crept into the kitchen in her stockinged feet. She saw us, turned around, and disappeared into the bedroom. She was fiercely silent during lunch, hardly looking up from her plate, and cleared the table as soon as our guests had put down their cutlery. She insisted on driving and sat impatiently behind the wheel, staring into space as I loaded the luggage into the boot. With her eyes glued to the road, she drove off in the wrong gear, jerking and shuddering away from Court Green, while I stayed behind with the children.

Perhaps it wasn't even the infatuation itself, but the decision to heed its devastating joy that led me for the first time in months toward poetry—my heart. Driven by the adventurous recklessness of the trickster, by the profound longing to put myself on the line, to lose all domestic certainties, I wanted nothing more than to be eviscerated by this black muse. Moreover, my wife, emerging from the cocoon of a false self, let the pain of love's loss course through her pen. She wrote two poems the day after the Wevills left, which to my dismay unabashedly addressed the subject of our marital woes. She placed the poems in front of me like an indictment. The cry from the heart—Who has torn us limb from limb?—cut me to the core, and the truth of our crippled contact paralyzed me with impotence. In the six years of our marriage, I had become lost in my devotion to the birth of this poetic self. Now that she had found her voice, and I needed to liberate mine from this form of worship, we were drifting apart. She wanted to go to the beloved father, and I wanted to return to reality, to nature, to my nature. Until the day she died, I believed that our estrangement was temporary, that—reborn, sadder, and wiser—we would find each other again. And I thought we had all the time in the world.

She was angling for the power of her first resurrection and believed she'd get closer to her father by keeping bees. In early June we drove to a meeting of beekeepers at Charlie Pollard's, gathered in an orchard around the hives with a number of beekeepers from the area, and—frightened to death—became members of this curious sect. Everyone had brought along appropriate clothing except us, the uninitiated. Someone loaned us outfits, and—masked and uniformed—we became an unrecognizable married couple among the other twosomes. With her characteristic determination, my wife swallowed her fear and gratefully accepted the old beehive that Charlie offered us. Back home I scoured and painted the small wooden castle while she applied hearts, flowers, and bluebirds to the white background and boned up on apiculture and the behavior of bees. On the 15th of June, we waited anxiously for the arrival of the hybrid colony. Dressed in a habit, hidden behind a veil, equipped with gloves and a censer full of smoke, with the beekeeper's help, she fitted the eight frames of furious insects into the wax house. I watched from a safe distance, without the protection of shrouds or smoke, and admired the mercurial energy with which she could lose herself in an activity. The first bee to sting me marked me as an enemy, and with that sounded the alarm for a small army of fanatic maniacs to open the attack, to sacrifice their lives for the protection of their queen by jabbing their stingers into my head. She saw me waving my arms wildly, pulled off her hood, and ran shrieking toward me to drive off the seething swarm.

I've saved the pocket diary from her last year, and now, thirty-five years after her death, I can't look at it without being touched by the hurtling anxiety with which she tried to rein in time. She planned her days to the minute, made note of what she'd do when, which tasks she'd set herself—type carbon copy of T.'s collection, send three poems to A. A., letter to mother—which chores she had to do—scrubbing, polishing, baking, errands, gardening—the time slot allotted to listening to radio programs—Bach, Beethoven, *Keep Up Your German*—what she'd cook that evening, when she'd wash her hair. With the exception of an entry in April—in which she noted with an exclamation mark that she'd started on her next novel—the mornings were blissfully blank. Following the Wevills' visit, a new task—handiwork—was added, generally timed to coincide with a radio program she wanted to listen to. A few days after their departure, our inauspicious visitor had sent my wife a small package containing all the materials needed for embroidering a miniature of roses. During her visit to Court Green, she'd admired the rag rug my wife was working on, made from worn pullovers and dresses cut into strips, carefully salted away for years like the camouflage of a wrathful self, now fearlessly destroyed and transformed into material for interwoven snakes rolled into a round carpet. While my wife plaited, I read aloud from Conrad's *Heart of Darkness*. I was under the impression that we were enjoying a distance that could still be bridged by our familiarity, until, after her death, I read in her journal that she'd invested her interweaving of the colorful strips of wool with a warmongering rage, and the purpose of the rag rug was no longer for prayer, but had become a carpet of fury.

She had waited for the post with more agitation than usual since the American release of *The Colossus* on May 14, anxious for an envelope from the publisher containing a review clipping. When my parents and uncle visited Court Green during the first week of June, she still hadn't received a single critique. She pinned all her hopes on the arrival of her mother, who from June 21 would be spending six weeks in our new home, and who might surprise us with a clipping from one of the Boston-area papers. But no matter what gifts Aurelia fished out of her voluminous trunk—along with my wife's sorely missed Americana—there was no review to be found.

For the first time, Aurelia held the grandson whose cranky entrance into the world had been more than made up for with a surplus of ready grins. His solipsistic chortling regularly startled every adult in the vicinity into subconsciously feeling he'd seen right through them.

In retrospect, Aurelia's visit to Court Green—seeing Frieda again, who had no trouble recognizing her grandmother and expressed it in a comically hysterical way, and meeting Nicholas—must have remained for her a sinister mix of a promising future and a past which was gone for good. Those six weeks, when she kept an overwrought, frightened eye on her daughter's every move, were to be the last weeks she'd ever spend with her. And in those weeks—in which her child would crow that she'd never been happier, and repeat dangerously often the mantra that Court Green was paradise, and she had everything she'd ever longed for, a magnificent husband, two adorable children, and her work—Aurelia would get to know the vindictive daughter, the one she'd later only encounter in a novel and in the poems.

In late June, my wife and I took the train to London, where we each had a recording session for a radio program in separate studios. We said goodbye on the platform and agreed to meet there later in the afternoon. I knew the address of the advertising agency where Assia worked as a copywriter, hailed a cab after the rehearsal, and raced with a pounding heart—almost breaking out of my rib cage—to the building on Berkeley Square, where I was told she'd just popped out on an assignment. I left a note saying I wanted to see her, in spite of the marriages. I didn't sign it. The next day a wordless letter arrived in the mail. When I opened the envelope I picked up the scent of Dior—she'd anointed a blade of grass. I plucked an identical blade from the banks of the Taw, equally long and green, and hoped it smelled of the earth, air, and water. I added it to hers, and sent them both back to her work address.

I had started an affair.

I didn't know that a sneering god, or some drunken mythographer, was splitting his sides at my folly and had thought up a shadow play, leading his hero, blinded by lustful passion, into an almost identical script so he'd commit all the same errors twice, only to then rob him of his beloved in the same horrific manner.

Nothing had happened yet. I'd written to her, phoned a few times, and we'd met for tea during a follow-up visit to London. My wife had just returned from an afternoon's shopping with her mother in Exeter when the phone in the hallway started to ring. She answered, heard a woman trying to drop her voice an octave so as to sound like a man, instantly recognized the throaty warble of our visitor, and called me. I ran down the stairs, stumbled, fell, clambered up, and, on the phone, was as terse as possible while my ashen-faced wife looked on like an infantryman, seconded by Aurelia. Grinning with embarrassment and awkwardness about this clichéd tableau, I hung up. Without saying a word, my wife yanked the phone's cable from the wall, ran up the stairs, and slammed the bedroom door. I found her crying on the bed, lay down beside her, took her in my arms, and confessed that I was in love, that for months I'd been gasping for air, that something inside me was dying, had been trussed up, asphyxiated, monitored, strangled by everything the little hearts she'd painted throughout the house represented, something that no longer had anything to do with our love but had become sentimental—a spell to counter her fears, or magical hex signs intended to ensure that everything remained as it was, the way she'd planned it, so she could contain her magnificent husband and adorable children within the heart-painted threshold. Moreover, that it was my own fault, I said, that I'd been ignoring the fox in my head for too long. We stayed upstairs for hours, talking, crying, trying to understand ourselves, and were disturbed only when Aurelia knocked and, obsequiously hunched, brought in a ravenous Nicholas.

The next day she ordered me to leave. After breakfast we retreated to the orchard to escape Aurelia's prying gaze, picked up the previous evening's discussion where we'd left off, were caught, crying, by Frieda, and decided that talking was getting us nowhere. We each needed to follow our own path for a while. To her, I'd fallen from my pedestal. The man she'd worshipped and adored, whom she'd placed above herself in every respect, was, in the end, the same as all the others—a liar, an adulterous cheat, a little man. She spat out the last words with so much contempt that it stung, and I snarled back that at least there was still one god she could turn to with her pathological desire for worship, and I knew for sure he was better equipped to withstand her sinusitis, migraines, mysterious fevers, hysterical bouts of crying, panic attacks, morbid jealousy, possessiveness, and especially that radioactive gleam in her eye. I immediately regretted the outburst but was too stubborn to take it back. She took me to the station, accompanied by Aurelia and the children, where, relieved, I bid farewell to a mother-in-law who was getting on my nerves and an icy wife who tensed every muscle, making clear I should make no attempt to touch her. I got on the train to London with a hastily stuffed bag, guilty, confused, and excited. The fire was burning and I could no longer put it out. I'd called Al Alvarez from a phone box in the village, explained the situation, and gratefully accepted his offer to let me sleep on his sofa. I could stay as long as I wanted.

I was able to piece together what happened next partly from what she told me herself, partly from the letters from Aurelia, and partly from the biographies. How, once back at Court Green, she went to my attic room and stuffed as many pages of notes, scribbled jottings, and letters as she could into a basket and carefully wiped down the work surface to collect any stray hairs or flakes of skin, grabbed the manuscript of her new novel from her own workroom, hauled the spoils down to the courtyard, threw them in a heap, and set it ablaze. She danced around the roaring flames and muttered unintelligible incantations and magical spells, poked the pyre with a stick, and seemed to be in a trance. A deeply concerned Aurelia watched from a distance and tried to restrain her granddaughter, who was irresistibly drawn to the fire. The only thing my wife had said was that her husband was having a thing with someone else. One scrap of paper drifted intact from the ashes of the burnt letters and poems and landed at her feet. She stooped, picked it up, and read the name of her rival. After that she took Nicholas from her mother, said she had to get away from here, that she was going to a friend's and wouldn't return until tomorrow morning. She drove to Elizabeth Compton, who lived with her family at a distance of some twenty miles, knocked on her door, and cried that she'd gone dry, that she had no more milk to feed her son. About that same time, I was ringing the Wevills' doorbell on Chalcot Square in London. I'd bought four bottles of champagne and told the astonished couple I was there to celebrate my birthday.

It was the beginning of July.

I only understood much later just how deranged I was at that moment.

How many years ago was it now, when, on a Friday the thirteenth, my bride rang the bell at 18 Rugby Street and became mine? The six years seemed like both an eternity and the blink of an eye. On Friday, July 13, 1962, I brought my Lilith to a hotel and used all my pent-up, dark electricity to tear the clothes from her body and take her. I didn't think about my wife, or about her husband, my children, or the future. The only thing I wanted was to obey the siren call of this black muse and everything that was dark and forbidden. I wanted to flout the civil laws which I'd imposed upon myself in marriage, experience the pleasure that I had denied myself, stop violating my nature. During our conversations, she'd given me the impression that her marriage to her Adonis had evolved over the years into a fraternal relationship, tender, sweet, and sexless. She phoned David from our hotel room to say she'd be home late because she first had to take me to the station. That led me to believe they had an open marriage in which they tolerated each other's affairs, and I was totally unprepared for the drama that was to unfold later that same night. Around midnight, while I was in the Tube heading back to my billet at Al Alvarez's, she returned home to Chalcot Square to find her husband passed out on the couch, an empty bottle of sleeping pills beside him on the floor. She rang the ambulance and spent the night with him in hospital. The next day, my wife reached me at Alvarez's and cryptically said she'd driven off the road, leaving open to doubt whether she'd had a blackout or had intended to take her own life. I returned to Devon immediately. Aurelia must have realized that her constant servile proximity prompted a great deal of physical revulsion in me, and she moved in with a neighbor and avoided us as much as possible during the day.

On August 4 we said goodbye to her from the station at Exeter. In the notes included in the publication of her daughter's letters—an edition that was meant to refute the disconcerting portrait of the mother in *The Bell Jar*—she wrote about the last time she saw her child, how nobody smiled except little Nicholas. On the way back to Court Green, my wife cried in shame about what her mother had witnessed, her failure as a spouse, as a mother, but before we'd arrived at our house, the humiliation had turned to rage and she said she didn't want to lay eyes on her mother in the coming years, because she hated her for the mortification she now felt. A fire burned in the garden a few days later. Hundreds of her mother's letters went up in smoke.

I'd reached a point of no return. The overwhelming pleasure of breaking out of the marriage was too liberating for me to climb back over the fence and voluntarily shackle myself to the role of magnificent husband. And I held firm to the belief that my wife also needed to be released from the subjugation of too much intimacy, that she'd arrived at a stage in her life and work in which she'd finally found the voice we'd so long searched for together. We decided that, as of November, we'd go our separate ways for six months, as far from each other as possible, and see how it went. I intended to spend some months in Spain, and my wife wanted to get away from Court Green for a while to live on the Irish coast, near the ocean. We found a sitter for the kids and travelled together to Yeats's country in search of rented accommodation. We were staying with Richard Murphy, a poet we'd met at one of the many poetry festivals. My wife had been on a jury that had recently awarded his work a prize. He had rooms to rent in his house on the coast and organized boat tours. My wife spoke about him flirtatiously, which only served to reassure me. I hoped he also had eyes for her so I could leave her behind with the reassurance that the winter for her in Connemara wouldn't be all too lonely. I didn't consider this Irish poet a rival any more than I viewed my black muse as the destroyer of our marriage. The only rival I had to contend with was death, and death was a one-legged Prussian bee king called Daddy.

I left at her request, a day after the three of us visited Yeats's tower in Ballylee. Murphy had driven us there in a van reeking of fish. My wife was in the passenger seat, and I had wormed my way into the back with the fifteen-year-old helper, talking with the lad about hunting and fishing while now and then I could pick up shreds of the conversation about our marital problems. My wife spoke with her familiar emphasis, loud and clear, and I noticed from the subdued voice with which Murphy responded that he was uncomfortable with the revelations concerning adultery and the lies being told within my hearing.

The rectangular tower Yeats had restored for his wife, George, stood untouched by time on the banks of a small stream, beside an elegant old bridge, a bastion of silence and concentration, high, mighty, with hardly any windows. We climbed a spiral staircase from floor to floor until we reached a tiny door at the top of the tower and were able to peer out from behind the stone ramparts over the rolling green landscape that he'd roamed and lauded. At the top of the tower, carried on a gentle September breeze, we poets brought an ode to William Butler Yeats by taking turns declaiming his verses. I listened with pain in my heart to my wife, who, in a somber voice with no outbursts or exaggerations, recited "Never Give All the Heart" and held my gaze during the last lines:

And who could play it well enough
If deaf and dumb and blind with love?
He that made this knows all the cost,
For he gave all his heart and lost.

I didn't know if her tears were elicited by the wind or the poetry, but—grief-stricken by powerlessness and pity—I threw an arm around her and could suddenly feel what I had so clearly seen but didn't want to admit, that she'd become thin as a rail. She asked for three coins, which I fished out of my pocket and handed to her. One by one she tossed them over the railing into the river, devoutly murmuring a wish for each.

"Yeats will look after me," she muttered.

She told me to leave, that my proximity hurt her too much. She felt comfortable with Murphy, and she'd continue her search for winter lodgings with him. So I left her behind on the coast of Connemara and drove south in the hired car. I drove out of our marriage, away from myself as a fantastic husband, out of our lives. Throughout the entire journey, the hands clasping the steering wheel could recollect the feeling of the butterfly-shaped wings of her shoulder blades, frail as a child's, and I gave that child—the eight-year-old girl dancing for her dying father to keep him alive with her bounteous love—back to the ocean. If I hadn't been convinced that we had both reached the point in our quests that we needed to face alone, that as a woman and a poet she had acquired an independence that made her strong enough to battle her demons without me, I never would have left. I understood from the previous months' poems that she needed to break free from me as much as I did from her. As frightened as I was by their personal nature, I realized at the same time that she'd liberated her brilliant and poetic self, unprecedented, new, original, shocking. The bell jar had been lifted, tortured Panic could shriek her note, and I could deliver myself from the straitjacket of being a father and a god rolled into one.

I didn't realize that Panic's song was as caustic as vitriol, barricading every conceivable love and compassion with a flaming hatred; that she'd use words as if they were a whetted ax to hack into the souls of her loved ones, to wound them as deeply and irreparably as she could. I had no idea that this blistering fury would be the very reason future generations of women would place her on a barbed throne, declaring her relentless voice the gospel of their own patricide, matricide, and spousal murders, deifying her and revering her as an icon of ruthlessness.

The moment I drove away from my marriage, I was declared an outcast, a character others could accuse and vilify to their heart's content, and the person leading this hot pursuit was my own wife. The first inkling of what my future would hold reached me via my parents. Shortly after my departure, they'd received some hate mail from their daughter-in-law in which their son was depicted as an adulterous liar and a hypocritical traitor who had abandoned his family in a most cowardly fashion to give full rein to his infantile, irresponsible, egotistical sexual appetites in London, where he'd taken up with a whore who, afraid of losing her fleshly beauty, had aborted so many pregnancies from her parade of lovers and husbands that she was now as infertile as a patch of barren ground. In the meantime she'd been left all alone to care for two small children—their very own grandchildren, mind—and their son had intentionally lured her away from the city, safely concealing her in this backward hinterland where she was deprived of any help or assistance from friends or family, while her faithless husband—now lionized for his poetry thanks to her ceaseless efforts—spent money in London earmarked for his family's support, squandering it on expensive hotels, women, champagne, and caviar.

My mother said she had burst into tears when she read the spiteful accusations, wanted to rush to her immediately, but was housebound by her arthritis. She'd urged my father to undertake the journey to Devon, but he was so unsettled by the hostile tone of the letters he didn't dare meet her face-to-face.

When she returned to Court Green, she found the telegram I'd sent from London saying I'd be away for fourteen days. I'd neglected to specify our destination, afraid she would follow me, and travelled with my Lilith—who'd fed her husband some cock-and-bull story about visiting family in Canada—to Spain, spent ten days enjoying her beauty and the ease with which she could make friends with a man, remained unsure about our future, and headed back to Devon. During the two weeks of my absence—supported by rustled-up reinforcements—my wife had hardened and become rigidly fixed in her martyr role. She fluttered the aerogrammes she'd received from her mother, the psychiatrist, the benefactress; quoted the rancorous advice from the keening furies—Free yourself from him! Hit him in the wallet! Throw him out of your bed!—and said she wanted a divorce.

I drove along the A30 back to London in a borrowed car, confounded, confused, blind to the autumn shedding its golden glow over the last days of September 1962. I knew that the moon in her seventh house made her sensitive to the influence of the fairy godmothers, who, full of veiled schadenfreude, saw a marriage that had seemed made in heaven suddenly hit the rocks and, to their unspeakable joy, appeared vulnerable to destruction. Although the excitement about my recaptured freedom hadn't disappeared, too much was happening over which I had no control, something I found sordid and frightening. Now that the sheath of our marriage had been torn, we were suddenly handed over to the malicious voices we'd been able to ignore as long as we'd been riveted together by love. The bloodthirsty hounds slipped in through the cracks, the ones I had been able to protect her from as long as I was by her side. Because I still believed a divorce would be premature, something neither of us wanted. I had no idea I was heading for a future in which the slobbering pack had set their sights on us and were tirelessly on the hunt for her posthumous existence, and my real daily life.

Dazed and guilty I'd walked into a trap with open eyes, probably because I so wanted to believe that she had indeed discarded her false selves. She took riding lessons, bought new clothes, changed her hairstyle, wrote as one possessed—glowing with an ecstatic fever of creativity—and I had faith in the resurrection. I'd heard through the grapevine that she boasted about throwing me out and now hailed her life without me as the happiest ever. Meanwhile I was leading a nomadic existence in London, staying here and there, rendezvousing with my married concubine during stolen hours, seeing other women, working harder than I'd worked in a long time, and missing above all the day-to-day contact with my daughter. I drove to Devon in early October to spend a few days sorting through my most important things. I played with Frieda, cared for Nicholas if she wanted to work, and slept in the attic. By day we avoided each other as much as we could—every conversation turned into an argument. Once we'd eaten and the children were asleep, she was too tired to dig up the hatchet again. Before I went to bed, I listened as she read her new poems aloud in an uncharacteristically monotonous voice, impressed by their brilliance and disturbed by their caustic, autobiographical nature. Here and there a sentence would sound like a snarl, uttered with the same sinister growl that had rattled me throughout my marriage. Defiant, she made no effort to hide the fact that she'd used my most recent work as scrap paper and written her poems on the back of verses she'd stolen from my room, traces of which showed through her handwriting like a palimpsest. From time to time I recognized the meter of my own poetry, especially in the one about the bee meeting, in which she sneeringly mocked me and at the same time gave me a cryptic warning that my flight from the marriage would land her in her coffin. I was too jaded by her victimhood to take the threat seriously and thought the lampoon a legitimate attempt to ridicule my escape.

In the years following her death and now—now that I'm trying to fill the void left by her suicide with poetry, carrying out a posthumous dialogue instead of a discussion that's no longer possible, completing the eighty-eight birthday letters to my bride to lay claim to my version of our love, affirming my rightful ownership of my memories, and allowing the poetic version of her story to be echoed in mine—the image often comes back to me of how we sat for the last time together by the fire in the crimson sitting room, and how the flames' glow clearly showed our words merging; one body, one spirit, a marriage of language.

By the time I left Court Green and she drove me to the station in a car loaded with carrier bags and sacks, I'd agreed to a divorce. Without abandoning hope of a reconciliation, I left her and the children behind that first week of October in a blazing Eden, where she bravely engaged in a lonely battle with the monsters, the pain, her anger and fears, with her daddy and mummy and with me, the man who, like her father, had also forsaken her. But the do-or-die fight, the one she carried out with her most trusted, inner other, was with a shadow self that demanded her life as a sacrifice and would only be satisfied with her death as the ultimate offering on the altar of love.

The literary world in London was abuzz with rumors and gossip. Everywhere I went, friends and acquaintances fell momentarily silent and then—like accomplished Iagos—passed along tales they'd picked up hither and yon, full of distorted truths and insinuations. Apparently there was a detective on my tail asking acquaintances the details of my actions and place of residence, the names of women, how much money I spent and on what; it seems that other friends—or especially the wives of friends—had been deployed by my wife as spies to check up on me and my lover and to feed her daily accounts of every step I took, every word I spoke. The treacherous whisperings in sitting rooms were just precursors of a hurricane of backbiting, rumors, slander, and defamatory exegeses that would raise its ugly head and pursue me to every corner of the earth for the rest of my life, gale-force winds chilling me to the bone.

Although she'd begged me to die or disappear so that she didn't have to breathe the same air as me, we kept up telephone contact about the children, maintenance payments, Court Green. As the weeks passed, the monotony disappeared from her voice—she sounded stronger, more mature, more independent. A friend helped her find a young nurse to look after the kids during the day and do some of the housework. She told me that in the hours before the children awoke—once she'd washed away the sleeping pills with copious amounts of coffee—she worked on an unending stream of poems, one every day, "book poems" as she liked to call them, each one better than the last. She'd given up on her idea of spending the winter in Ireland and wanted to rent a flat in London. That's where her friends lived; she wouldn't be so cut off from libraries, museums, and theaters; she could start her longed-for literary salon, and the childcare and visitation agreements would be easier to arrange.

After camping out on the sofa in Al Alvarez's studio and spending a number of weeks in the flat of Dido Merwin's recently deceased mother, I moved into a place in Soho, a fixed address that all the same wouldn't stick and had the temporary character of something in transit, even though I had no idea where I was heading. As much as I hankered after the warmth of my Lilith's nearness, what gave me the greatest joy in those days was the slowly returning sensation that my nerves were reconnecting with my soul.

To my delight, my wife agreed to let me help her find a flat. I surveyed the to-let adverts posted on notice boards in Underground stations, wrote down some addresses, picked her up at friends', and spent hours walking through the city with her. She searched with her trademark inexhaustible energy and perseverance, was witty and cheerfully sparkling, and she reminded me of the woman I had married six and a half years earlier. With the exception of the occasional gibe, she no longer went on like a broken record about the lies, betrayal, and infidelity; the affair with the barren bitch to whom—for all she cared—I could go ahead and become the fourth husband in a row; or the harem I was secretly maintaining, talentless star-hunters who were delighted to get involved with the handsome, famous, virile poet and, in so doing, dupe his famous wife. She talked instead about poems, publications, a request to collaborate on a festival for American poets in the coming summer, the commission from the BBC to write about her childhood, her future in London, interesting friendships. With a smile as mysterious as she could muster—one she couldn't quite pull off—she said she'd found in Al Alvarez a friend and confidant to whom she could read her poems aloud, and he, with his expertise, enthusiasm, and boundless admiration for what he heard, gave her enormous encouragement by convincing her that she, like Emily Dickinson, was one of the greatest American poetesses ever. If she wanted to hurt me, she said that Frieda was suffering because of the separation and was slowly evolving from a chipper, alert little girl into a child with a broken wing. Nicholas was too young to pick up on what was happening and still too attached to her to even miss me. Moreover, she said, I'd avoided baby Nick from the word go, probably out of a fear of masculine competition and—infected as I was by all those Celtic, Greek, and God-knows-what-all myths—apprehensive of the day he'd try to dethrone me. She couldn't have been more wrong, but pleased as I was with this fragile reconciliation, I didn't rise to the bait of her accusations, let her vent her spleen, said nothing.

She found 23 Fitzroy Road with the help of Yeats. She'd practically cut off the top of her thumb, neglected the wound, worried about gangrene, and finally went to see Dr. Horder in Primrose Hill. After the appointment in our old neighborhood, she walked along her favorite street, was pulled by some magical power to the poet's house, and discovered a to-let sign at number 23. Trembling with excitement, she asked the workmen renovating the building if she could look at the two top floors, raced up the stairs, realized at once that this was what she was looking for, and went to a phone box to call first the estate agent and then me. I promised to help, arranged things so she could pay the rent a year in advance, and allowed her to put me down as her husband because, as a single mother, she had little chance.

Every Thursday at ten o'clock, I rang the bell at 23 Fitzroy Road to pick up the children and take them to the zoo, or to spend a few hours playing with them on the blue painted floor of the sitting room. We'd spent Christmas apart. I'd invited her and the children to come with me to the Beacon, but she said—lied—she had plans with someone. Although I knew her as a woman of appalling exaggerations, I was not yet accustomed to her falsehoods, so I trusted she was speaking the truth, indulged her amorous undertone, didn't bother about the who and what. It was only during the first week of the new year, when Al Alvarez, with amicable intimacy, told me about his Christmas Eve visit to her, that I lamented my restraint. She'd rung and asked him to come to dinner that evening. He'd had to turn her down because friends in the neighborhood were expecting him, but he promised to drop in for a drink along the way. He said he was taken aback when she opened the door. The usually fresh and lively woman, always as carefully coiffed as a schoolmarm, stood there like an emaciated priestess, her unwashed hair hanging in greasy strands around her pale gray face. She trudged up the stairs ahead of him. The only semblance of the woman he remembered was the gleam in her eye as soon as she sat cross-legged on the straw mat and read her poems aloud. He couldn't say for sure if it was the extreme poetry that took his breath away, or her loneliness which, in spite of her recovered bravura, filled every corner of the room. Around eight he announced he was leaving for his next engagement. When he told me how she then burst into tears and begged him not to leave her on her own, it was as if he plunged a knife into my heart.

Eight years after her death, he would publish his reminiscences of that Christmas Eve—slightly reformulated and leaving out the heart-rending detail about her entreaties—in the *Observer*, under the controversial headline, "Sylvia Plath: The Road to Suicide." The following exciting installment of the tragedy was announced in a screaming banner as if it were some sordid tabloid cliff-hanger: "NEXT WEEK: The Last Gamble."

The children were eleven and nine. Until then, I had managed to shield them from their mother's suicide. When the *Observer* appeared on the newsstands, I picked them up from boarding school and spent several days trying to help them understand something incomprehensible. I wrote a high-handed letter to the traitor, rang the newspaper, managed to block the publication of the second installment, but could not prevent his book about suicide appearing a month later. Alvarez introduced *The Savage God* with a dramatic account of my wife's last days, including all the horrific details I would have preferred to keep from my children, and pontificated about her suicide with his pseudo-psychology bunkum.

It was November 1971, our friend had turned a deaf ear to my pleas for clemency, disregarded my fears about the power of the word and the disastrous impact his reporting would have on the children's lives, and with his rancid, melodramatic memoirs left the door wide open to the divine judgment of a hysterical horde which, from that moment on, would hunt for a scapegoat, taking up a never-ending pursuit.

In the last week of December 1962, the winter was already displaying its cosmic power to disrupt orderly life. It was to become the harshest winter England had seen in one hundred and fifty years and—in that catastrophic screenplay in which one disastrous occurrence is piled on top of the other—it still needed another six and a half weeks to become one of Fate's most impassive accomplices.

I drove to Devon the week after Christmas to pick up the red curtains my wife had asked for. The A30 was glass-slick from the encrusted snow and sleet, so it took me twelve hours to cover the two hundred miles back to the house where I had left her—and a part of myself—behind. When I arrived, the stained-glass windows of the church captured the sinking sun. There was still just enough light to dig the potatoes out of their subterranean straw bed, to sort through the apples in the outbuilding and fill two sacks for her. With the displaced sensation that I was robbing myself, I crept like an intruder through the silent, woolly, snow-wrapped house. A bluish twilight glow gave familiar objects a ghostly illumination, and I could hear nothing but our absence.

In January it snowed incessantly. The country had ground to a halt because of frozen and burst pipes, overtaxed power stations failing left and right, leaving the city in medieval darkness, trains frozen onto the rails, lorries engulfed in snow, shortages in the shops, hospitals over-flowing with hypothermic pensioners. Nature had spared nothing in bringing us to our knees. I relished the challenge of survival in such harsh circumstances, but my pleasure was dampened by my worries about my wife and children. She still hadn't installed a telephone, was often without heat and warm water, had the greatest difficulty making her way outdoors with little Frieda and Nicholas in the pram to buy groceries, took an eternity to reach the shops and then—laden and encumbered—to head back to Fitzroy Road. Whenever she needed to place a call, she and the children had to join the long queue in the icy cold outside a phone box. In order to help her, I had to pierce through the facade of pride and deference she used to maintain the pretense of happiness, autonomy, and a lavish circle of friends. Thanks to the web of scouts, spies, and messengers in which I had become entangled, I knew who her most important new friends were because these were also the intimates of my gossip-mad Lilith, for whom my wife's charade—suggesting a triumphant victory—was intended, and who for her part made sure that everything she said reached my wife's ears.

When all three of them were in bed with the flu, I rang Dr. Horder. He called at Fitzroy Road that very day, was shocked by the deplorable state of my wife, prescribed nutritional supplements and sleeping pills, and arranged, via the National Health Service, a nurse's daily assistance. I now visited my family a few times a week, bringing her tea in bed, trying to get Frieda to drink an entire glass of orange juice, giving Nicholas his bottle and resisting—as cold-bloodedly as I could—that pair of blazing brown eyes and my daughter's crying when, after a few hours, I left. There was none of the usual bickering and when she was feeling well enough, I bought a bottle of champagne to celebrate how well we were getting along again. By mid-January her recovery was sufficient for her to attend a modest reception for *The Bell Jar* at her publisher's. I accompanied her. She was hoping—as Victoria Lucas—to cash in with the book, she said, and didn't seem burdened by any scruples over the merciless portrayals of her mother, benefactresses, and friends, which could now be read by all. She didn't mention that a week earlier, her American publisher had turned down the novel and had sent back almost all the *Ariel* poems—with the exception of the least aggressive. There she stood, pale and emaciated, holding on to the account of her first suicide, trying to ignore the signs that history was repeating itself and that she was again losing her grip on reality, and on herself.

She said she could handle it, that it would do her good to see where I lived, to give reality a chance to govern the fantasy she was now hopelessly subjected to. I had given her my phone number but had kept the address to myself, still on the run, afraid she'd stand guard in front of the house like a jailer or barge in unexpectedly to catch me in the act, perpetrating my next crime. I haltingly agreed and revealed the location of my lair, in order not to jeopardize the growing—and still gossamer-like—friendship between us.

On Tuesday, February 5, she ventured out into snow-covered London, rang the bell around noon, and I let her into the house that had never offered me shelter, a storeroom full of boxes and carrier bags. Everything in this room had a provisional air, with the exception of the table full of books, notepads, and sheets of paper covered in handwriting. She did exactly what I'd been dreading, leaving me ashamed of her and of me. Without the slightest reservation, she poked around like a trained bloodhound, snooping for signs betraying the existence of the woman whose name she hadn't spoken since driving her back to the station at Exeter. Like a shot, with a feverish gaze, she registered that there were no traces on the bed, among the clothes draped over a chair, or on the table. Tired, sick, and relieved, she called off the hunt. In fits and starts she began telling me about the panic attacks, the antidepressants she'd been taking for a few days now, the disappointing reactions to *The Bell Jar*, and the humiliation she'd had to endure when, on the very page in the *Observer* where her novel was written off with a couple of lines, there appeared a prominently printed poem of mine, "Full Moon and Little Frieda," for crying out loud, as if the child didn't belong to both of us.

Even as a mother, she had to remain under my shadow. Without catching her breath, she rattled on about what she'd heard from her girlfriends, that the nasty witch and I hoped she'd do herself harm so we'd be rid of her and could go our merry way unhindered; that in any case the childless bitch bad-mouthed her to all and sundry, and I must have made her out to be a jealous, egotistical, narcissistic, manipulative hysteric who increasingly resembled her bigoted mother, kept me on a short leash for years in a suffocating marriage, and blackmailed me with the children; and that her girlfriends, bar none, advised her to divorce me double-quick because I was an incorrigible womanizer and she'd never be able to tame me. I denied everything, bowled over by the malevolence of the rumors, said she was being stoked by her so-called helpful friends with malicious lies, demanded to know their names, threatened to have a lawyer sue them for slander, and repeated what I'd said before, that I wanted to save our marriage but that she had to grant me more freedom; that in the course of the years, our intimacy had become destructive for us both and had quashed something valuable inside of us. I suggested we go somewhere together, away from the city, where we could hear each other without being interrupted by the wails and whispers of pernicious schemers, troublemakers, and meddlers. She saw that I was sincere, confessed that the whole divorce had been a bluff arising from wounded pride and stubbornness, from sorrow at the loss of our Eden, our perfect marriage, and asked me to trust her. Even though I didn't quite understand what she meant, I said I trusted her, and that yes, we would spend the coming summer reunited beneath the laburnum, I would do whatever she wanted, leave or stay, I was a parcel with only one address—ours. Just as she seemed convinced, she spied something in the room that wasn't quite right. The red Shakespeare printed on bible paper—the one she'd ripped to shreds in a jealous rage—was sitting on my writing table like a resurrected relic, a miraculous reappearance of a treasured object that had succumbed at a time when things—but not our love—could be destroyed. Wavering—as if she knew what she was about to put herself through—she went to the table and opened the book. My heart sank, because I knew the sweet words penned in wispy blue ink she'd find on the title page, signed by the woman whose name she would never utter again. She was standing with her back to me. I could tell by the cringing of her long neck that the dedication had—in the fraction of a second—dealt her a mortal blow.

It was never her intention that I'd receive it on Friday, but thanks to a bizarre twist of fate, Royal Mail delivered the farewell letter the same day she'd posted it. After reading the first few lines, I was so alarmed I sprinted to the Tube and, in no time, gasping for breath, rang the bell at Fitzroy Road, imagining her hanging from a noose or with slashed wrists. When she opened the door, I burst into tears of pure relief, surprised I had so much trouble staunching the stream, and was in no state to understand their premature portent. She led the way up the stairs, her thick hair luxuriously curled as if for a party. The flat was cold and empty, the children had been taken to stay with a couple she'd befriended. I pulled out the letter so she could clarify its contents, but before I knew what was happening, she snatched it from me, went over to the ashtray, struck a match, and burned it. She looked at me with a strange smile—calm, cruel, remote.

I can't say for sure what words she used to reassure me to the point where I left her alone that night. She must have denied—in her own scornful way—that it was a suicide note, that she'd gone to Fitzroy Road that afternoon without the children to commit suicide, a carefully considered plan thwarted by the mail service's sudden and unexpected efficiency and by the panic a final love letter, delivered too early, had triggered in her unfaithful husband. And I—numbed by this endless repetition—probably felt caged once again by her pathological neediness, and then rejected and humiliated by her smug pride.

I left.

Two days later I spent the night—which was to be the last night of her life—at the same address where our life together had begun, hiding in someone else's lavish locks from the drama that was taking place. Since my escape, Susan had become the only woman I could turn to when—torn between an Eve and a Lilith—I sought solace from my untamed love life. She wrote poetry, was an editor at my publisher's, had the sculpted beauty of a Renaissance Madonna, and her sweet, nonjudgmental friendship was as medicinal to me as madder root. I'd rung her—confused and distraught—on Sunday evening and asked to meet at our pub, The Lamb, told her about the letter and the burning of it, said I was tormented by a desperate restlessness, asked if she would spend the night with me, and perversely decided not to take her back to my flat as usual but to go to 18 Rugby Street, where, since her divorce, she'd lived on the top floor. Now that I'd revealed to my wife the location of my hideaway, I was suddenly afraid she'd surprise me at home after the weekend, to finally trap me in the early hours in someone else's arms, and all would be lost. I returned for the first time to our old address. In the ground-floor corridor, I again passed the door, opened just a crack, behind which, after all those years, the same resident hid, unchanged, held captive by an insane, barking Alsatian. I looked into the lovely, plump face of the young woman, who was astonished to see a ghost from the past, and who, in just three days, would become an anonymous player, another thread in the artistic tapestry that Fate was doggedly weaving, by gassing herself and her growling guardian.

In the early morning of Monday, February 11, 1963, ignorant of the calamity that had taken place at 23 Fitzroy Road, which was then just coming to light, I drove my friend to her office, went home, lit the fire, sat at my desk, and wrote. It was deceptively quiet for three long hours until around noon, when the telephone jolted me awake and shrilly tore the veil from my staggering naivety. I picked up the receiver only to be struck by the four devastating words that would echo through the rest of my life: "Your wife is dead."

An impenetrable shroud hangs over everything that took place in the hours and days that followed. What I clearly recall is that while I was aware of the irrefutable truth of the horrific news, knew for certain she had committed suicide, I simultaneously sprinted to the Underground with the same insane anxiety as two days before, in the hope that the script hadn't changed, that she would again open the door, surprised and satisfied with my tears, and that I, with my arrival, would twist the plot of a presaged tragedy. But a policeman opened the door. I followed him upstairs through a corridor smelling of gas and entered a sitting room full of whispering strangers. I searched for her, looked for the children, and asked anyone I saw to tell me where she was—still hoping I could forestall her death. Dr. Horder took me aside and explained— with an irritatingly powerless professionalism—what had happened in the preceding hours.

He said she was severely depressed—gauged my facial expression to see if I'd ever drawn the same conclusion—and had found her condition so worrying that he had tried to have her admitted to hospital before the weekend. He hadn't succeeded and therefore had remained in constant contact with her the last few days and had arranged for her to get some assistance today from a nurse. She knew that the nurse was due to arrive at nine in the morning. She arrived punctually, rang the bell, but wasn't admitted. Afraid she had the wrong address, she went to the phone box to call the agency, was reassured it really was 23 Fitzroy Road, went back, and finally, with some help from a workman, gained access to the house. They could smell a penetrating odor of gas in the hallway. They stormed up the stairs and broke down the kitchen door. My wife had stuffed the cracks with sheets and towels, put her head into the oven as far as it would go, and gassed herself. The plumber carried her to the sitting room, the nurse—although it was clearly futile—attempted mouth-to-mouth resuscitation, but it was too late. They heard the children crying upstairs. The door to their bedroom, like the one in the kitchen, had been blocked with rolled-up clothes and towels. The window was wide open and beside each little bed was a tumbler of milk and a plate of sandwiches. The children were chilled to the bone, but unharmed. A note was found downstairs in the hallway. It had been taped to the pram. There was a phone number on it and beneath that the words: PLEASE PHONE DR. HORDER. He'd rushed over immediately but could do nothing more for her. He believed she'd committed suicide around five or six o'clock in the morning.

"I want to go to her," I said.

It was still a few hours before I was allowed to see her, because an autopsy was being carried out. To quell the image of violation to a body whose every inch I knew, that I could still feel under my fingertips and had never stopped desiring, I withdrew with the children to their bedroom and allowed myself to be distracted by Frieda's jabbering and Nicholas's complicated smile. Someone had lugged an electric heater upstairs so we wouldn't freeze to death, but the cold had penetrated my bones and I had to use all my willpower to keep my teeth from chattering. My wife's room—which I'd never entered—was beside the children's. There was a cardboard sign hanging on a tack with the words: SILENCE! GENIUS AT WORK!

It was only in the afternoon that it really sunk in, once I was admitted to the hospital's mortuary. It wasn't so much the waxen honey-yellow color of the suddenly much narrower face that convinced me I couldn't save her from death, but the unusual inanimacy of that beloved visage from which all alertness and tension had evaporated. I'd never seen her at such peace, even in sleep. All of a sudden she resembled the little girl she must've been before her father died, when he was her Almighty, and she still lived in an inviolate kingdom. The only reminder of the life and suffering that began afterwards was the scar beneath her right eye, as if God's hand had accidentally slipped while he was carving her head out of marble.

Numbed by the shock, gutted and struck dumb by a wrenching pain, I walked out with a wedding ring, a watch, and a lock of hair. The Monday was dull gray, and London plowed forth as if the earth hadn't just capsized. While I wandered dazed through a forever-altered world, one sentence kept running through my head: I am guilty, I.

I considered her suicide a death with an addressee. Back at Fitzroy Road I ignored the visitors and searched high and low, looking for a letter in which she solved the riddle of her suicide, damned me or granted me absolution, one that convinced the children of her love so they'd be sure of it for the rest of their days, but the only things she'd left behind were a black ring binder with poems called *Ariel* that she'd dedicated to Frieda and Nicholas, stacks of loose sheets of poetry and prose, and the journals. In the kitchen, the oven, whose door still stood open, contained the folded towel on which she'd nestled her head. I even peered in there, in the hope she'd been clutching a message for us and had only let go once the gas sedated her and slackened her grasp on life. I used the towel to wipe away my tears and shut the oven door before the children were brought downstairs.

In the course of the week—without ever fully understanding what had pushed her over the edge—I was able to piece together the narrative of her final days from the mosaic of witness testimonies. The couple my wife had turned to for assistance were the first people Dr. Horder notified about her death, because no one had my phone number. They'd reached me through various channels. I rang Jillian and Gerry Becker that very Monday, asked them to come to Fitzroy Road, spoke a while with the good-natured man, ignored the wife's hostile glowering, and called them again a few times in the days that followed to fill in the gaps in the timeline.

On Thursday morning my wife, clearly desperate, had rung them asking if she could come over with the children. They'd known each other since my wife had moved to London, felt sorry for her, and, since then, had looked after her on a regular basis. No matter how shamelessly demanding she was, they enjoyed her company, the erudition, the astute observations, the amusing anecdotes, the juicy caricatures of friend and foe. She arrived half an hour after ringing, was for the first time openly at her wits' end, kept repeating how miserable she felt, hadn't brought along anything for the children or herself, asked if she could go to bed, and marched straight upstairs, where she slept for hours. They shared the same general practitioner, so they rang Dr. Horder and asked his advice. He was worried, said she had to keep taking her pills—especially in the morning when a dangerous dip in the drug-response curve could occur—and emphasized how crucial it was that she care for the children herself. She would be getting assistance as of Monday, and they should do everything in their power not to leave her alone before then. After she'd had a bath—the first of many in the coming days—she came downstairs miraculously revived, a completely different woman from a few hours earlier, ate dinner with gusto, but seemed oblivious to the children. Mrs. Becker drove to Fitzroy Road to pick up some clothes, nappies, and bottles for the children, and also, at my wife's request, two books, a makeup bag, a set of curlers, and her new evening gown. Although she felt uncomfortable, she let herself into the flat, went in search of the requested necessities, and found everything except clothes for Frieda. Even in the laundry basket, there was nothing. It gave her the shivers. They were used to my wife's moaning about being strapped for cash, but she'd never buy a new dress for herself and nothing for the children. She gently broached the subject when she got back. My wife ignored the concern about Frieda's lack of clothing and hinted that the dress had been a gift from a lover. They didn't believe her.

That first night, and all those that followed, my wife begged Jillian to stay with her until she fell asleep. Sitting on the edge of the bed, Jillian listened to endless tales of people she didn't know and the man-eating slut who'd stolen me, a devil my wife had summoned herself; she heard accusations aimed at me and at the sycophantic supporters who'd fed my ego, bitches and scoundrels who'd left her in the lurch, listened to bitter tirades about her mother's ambition, in whose eyes she'd failed now that her marriage was on the rocks and whom she hated because she made her feel ashamed. The woman was relieved and exhausted each time my wife finally stopped rambling and fell asleep. Three nights in a row she was woken after a few hours by a cry for help, which also woke the children. The friend then got them out of bed, brought them to her to calm them down, and, at my wife's bidding, sat with her again until she dozed off.

On Friday morning they'd taken her and the children to the zoo. My wife had posted a few letters and made an impression more of absence than of desperation. The oddest thing was she paid no attention to the children, no matter how often things like filthy nappies, hunger, or thirst were pointed out to her. She seemed to hear and see nothing.

In the course of the afternoon, she became increasingly agitated, packed her curlers and the dress into a valise, said she had an important appointment—she didn't say with whom—and took off in the Morris. They waited for hours, worried sick, and heaved a sigh of relief when, later in the evening, she turned up seeming calmer, as if the meeting had done her some good. But that night, the ritual of continuous talking, begging, reproaches, falling asleep, waking up in the middle of the night, crying out, and then more confused monologue was replayed all over again.

The next day they realized that she must have come home in a taxi because the Morris was nowhere to be found and, when asked where it was, she couldn't say.

On Sunday, something seemed to have changed. For the first time, she slept late, came downstairs more chipper than on the preceding days, enjoyed an early dinner, and announced she wanted to go home. They'd demurred, tried to put the idea out of her head, but she was adamant. Against his better judgment, the husband agreed to her request, drove the car around the front, and let my wife and children into the back seat. She'd cried the whole way.

Everyone assumed that the downstairs neighbor had gone to work in the morning as usual, but it turned out he was still in bed, unconscious from carbon-monoxide poisoning, and was only discovered that afternoon. Although I found him an unpleasant person—much like Mrs. Becker—I sought him out to ask if he had anything to add about the night before. She'd knocked on his door late in the evening, he said, and asked for some postage stamps. He'd gone to get some, at first refusing the money she'd brought along, but she insisted on paying so that she would have a clear conscience before God. Then she asked what time he'd be going to work the following morning. Eight thirty, he'd said. He said goodbye, closed the door, saw that the hall light was still on, and opened the door again. She stood frozen on the spot, gazing aloft as if in a trance. When he asked if he could do anything else for her, she brushed him off and said she'd just had a glorious vision. A little later he heard some stumbling on the stairs, and in the hours that followed, he could hear her upstairs, frantically pacing.

The strangers left, friends and family members arrived. My sister from Paris, my dark muse—who'd left her husband at home—my aunt and my cousin from Yorkshire, Lucas, Susan, Al Alvarez, Warren—who'd flown all the way over from the US with his brand-new wife. One by one, in the course of the week, with heavy hearts they entered the sitting room on Fitzroy Road, a place most of them had never been, which—no matter how crowded it became—continued to echo with a chilling emptiness. The moment I left her behind in the mortuary, I'd fallen out of life. For the most part, conversations washed over me, I was insensitive to physical contact, and while my soul was silenced, questions and images raced through my head. The only thing that reminded me of my physical existence was the keening pain in my neck and left shoulder that began when—in my mind—I hung myself by a hook attached to the muscle under my skull, naked prey for the guilt-vulture. I recalled "The Hanging Man" and how much it had upset me at the time. It was the first poem she'd written after Frieda's birth, but the two-lined stanzas shimmered with ominous threat. There was no trace of the maternal joy she had so longed for. I looked up the poem—her voice—as I was to do repeatedly in the coming weeks and months, saw that she'd included it in the *Ariel* collection, reread it, and cursed myself for the careless negligence that had kept me silent when she'd first read it aloud a fleeting three years earlier.

Al Alvarez had once made a serious attempt to take his own life, and so felt like a member of the club and put himself forward as an expert on suicide. He contested Dr. Horder's diagnosis that her suicide had been inevitable and insisted she hadn't wanted to die: an unfortunate series of coincidences had prevented her being snatched from the jaws of death in time. With her penchant for dangerous intensity, she'd risked all and been unlucky. The harsh, incessant winter, the recurring sinusitis, the care for the two children as a single mother—putting her in the same boat as her own mother after her father's death—the letter to a psychiatrist asking for emergency help that was delivered to the wrong address so she received no answer, the gas that had knocked out the downstairs neighbor, making him unable to open the door for the nurse or save her because he'd been alerted by the noxious odor in the corridor—it had been one huge conspiracy of Fate, intent on destroying her.

Out of deference, he kept the part I had played off his list, but I filled in the gaps myself.

Each day I dreaded the moment when the sitting room would slowly clear out, when friends would go back to their houses or hotels, our collective wake at an end. To everyone who entered, I read aloud her astonishing poems, written in blood, a slashed-open vein from which flowed her bitter yet hilarious "Daddy," "Fever 103°," the bee poems, "Ariel," and "Lady Lazarus." She had transformed her inability to write about anyone but herself into a driving force and, with a flaming tongue, set the soul of her true self on display. One evening my cousin tried to pull me out of grief's numbness by suggesting that I sing a song. I began "Waltzing Matilda" with a wavering voice and sang it from the first line to the last with tears pouring down my face. Thereafter, the ballad ran through my head day and night, I heard her hearty laugh when I sang "billy boiled" and "billabong," and how she begged me with childlike glee to sing it again and again.

The first night in her bed, I sniffed the sheets and pillows like an abandoned fox cub, searching for her nesting scent, which I detected only once I pressed a nightgown under my nose. After hours of tossing and turning, I'd sunk into a restless half sleep, when I was awoken by Frieda's crying. I got up and went to the nursery. While I rocked my daughter in my arms, all of a sudden I heard the wolves in the zoo answering her sobs with a wailing lament. The entire pack soon joined in with a woebegone chorus, howling for minutes on end to support us in our sorrow, trying to comfort us, as they would every night during the weeks that followed.

The official inquest took place four days after her death. I was called upon to identify my wife, and everyone who had been present in the initial hours after her demise was cross-examined by the magistrate. As if answering to divine judgment, I confirmed that the woman in the mortuary was indeed my lawful-wedded wife, Sylvia Plath Hughes, born on October 27, 1932, in Boston, Massachusetts, America, died on Monday, February 11, 1963, at 23 Fitzroy Road, London, England, writer, thirty years old, mother of Frieda Rebecca Hughes, a little more than two and a half, and Nicholas Farrar Hughes, thirteen months old. And yes, I was their father. The report about that fatal Monday was drawn up and the cause of death rubber-stamped. "Committed suicide." It was February 15, the feast of Lupercal. Back home, two abandoned children awaited her return, and they couldn't understand why for days they'd had to do without the devotion of their mother.

The inquest proved to be just the prologue to the opus in which, from that day forward, I would become the prime suspect, the subject of a never-ending investigation. The judge acquitted me. I didn't acquit myself.

On Sunday morning I got in beside the driver of the hearse containing the coffin and brought her home to the land of my heart, where we buried her on Monday, February 18, in the Calder Valley, in the snow-covered graveyard of Heptonstall, a stone's throw from the house where we'd spent many weeks together, celebrated Christmases, and where my parents—paralyzed with grief—were biding their time. I remember nothing of the brief church service, nor of the handful of visitors. I kept my gaze fixed on the coffin to stay as close to her as I could and fathom the absoluteness of her death. After everyone had tossed a shovelful of sand into the freshly dug hole, I asked them to leave me alone. The raw opening in the earth was illuminated by a watery February sun. I looked into the depths and scourged myself with images of her last night, imagined how she went outside in the dark, in her long black winter coat, the rolled-up plait pinned to her crown, dragging herself through the freezing cold to the phone box, exhausted, frightened, already almost a nonperson, to phone me, listening to the endless ringing and I wasn't there to answer, I was not there for her. To put an end to the pain, I gently sang the last verse of "Waltzing Matilda" to my bride and asked her to forgive all my wrongs.

I had sent the fateful telegram to Aurelia's sister so that someone would be with her when she was told the news of her daughter's death. I didn't have the heart to say she'd committed suicide and left it to Warren to fill her in on the details when he returned to America. But I suspect she knew right away and only kept up the pretense that her daughter had died from complications relating to pneumonia for the benefit of her family, friends, and the press. The Sherlock Holmes–like questions from Warren seemed to originate directly from her and were clearly intended to find out if the kids would be allowed to grow up in the US. Once she'd received official notification of the suicide, she could check up on me, bold as you please. Word reached me from every quarter that she'd phoned or written to the doctor, friends, acquaintances, and the divorce lawyer, to dig into my share in the tragedy, to find out if I was capable of looking after the children and what part the married mistress would play in their upbringing. I later found some letters from her mother among the earthly remains that had escaped the bonfire of liberation, whose contents exacerbated my dislike a great deal. They advised her to dump me posthaste so Aurelia could make a fresh start remolding her daughter for the prestigious marriage the child's ambitious upbringing had groomed her for all along. Aurelia's voice was just one among the choir of malignant females who, during the months of our mutual estrangement, had assailed my needy wife with disastrous advice, mutinous instructions, incriminating information, reported conversations, spied assignations. It seemed as if I had been followed everywhere and photographed, overheard, and bugged.

It unleashed a fury in me that served as an antidote to sorrow's inertia while at the same time lifting the lonely yoke of guilt, because I grew to see the swarm of hornets as being jointly responsible for her suicide. I don't know how long I held on to the naive assumption that the death of my wife would put an end to the slander and the defamatory chant would die down now they'd managed to drive one of us into the grave.

It was only the beginning.

For the past thirty-five years, I have been a silent hostage to her myth, locked in a mausoleum in which I was exhibited as the relic of a tragic marriage. We have entered the imagination of millions, joined at the hip, described by biographers, hagiographers, journalists, academics, and scholars of Scripture, with Daddy and Mummy as our witnesses; attached to each other like one another's shadow selves, linked characters in a passion play from which there was no escape, in which the roles were assigned thousands of years ago and the protagonists submissively obeyed the destiny prescribed for them.

From the moment of her self-chosen death, I inherited her language, became the executor of her posthumous fame, and thereby carried out my own sentence as executioner. By publishing *Ariel*, I'd given the world a noose with which to hang me—along with everyone she'd loved. Time, as in all tragedies, was a cunning antagonist due to the rise of militant feminism, embroiled in a holy war, in search of a god to worship and a scapegoat to punish. Down through the years, my public execution in the bullring has been accompanied by masses of screaming women waving banners with the word "Murderer!" The believers trekked to the Golgotha in Heptonstall, thrust the pens of their fury into the soil like swords around her grave, and time and again defaced the headstone by hacking my name off hers.

I often think back on the last week of her life when—ecstatic about discovering her poetic self—she said that God was speaking through her, and—alarmed—I clamped a hand over her mouth as if I could shove the blasphemous words back into silence. Because the fate of God's spokespeople is immutably tied to the ever-repeating destiny of desert saints, crusaders, jihadists, prophets, and witches: martyrs of the faith who—deeply convinced of their mission—rapturously end up on the cross or burned at the stake. I found the harrowing logic behind her yearning for sacrifice in countless passages in her journals. She'd written the most painful entry at Yaddo, when—newly pregnant with our first child—she stated that her long-standing wish was to be rewarded for her own elimination. No matter how much it hurt to read that, the deeply entrenched power of a sacred mandate forced me to realize that even motherhood could not have freed my wife from her own myth. No love could ever have been big enough to keep her from fulfilling the old laws of her father's testament. She gave her body for the Word, and the disciples still kneel every day before the altar of a life sacrificed to literature.

It's always the biggest hypocrites who claim, with sanctimonious indignation, that the dead can no longer defend themselves from blame and imputations, only to take aim at the nearest survivors and pump them full of bullets. As if the living are able to shield themselves from the hail of libel, slander, insinuations, and gossip; as if, as long as you are able to speak, there's some possibility of defending yourself from lies.

Biographers behave like they own your existence, as if it's a product. I rediscovered my stolen life in books; saw my love, marriage, feelings, thoughts, and actions interpreted by friends and strangers; read how facts were repudiated or distorted, how words that I had never uttered were put in my mouth, how I was assigned character traits I simply do not possess. Complete strangers—journalists and researchers intent on lining their pockets—used our names with an impudence that made my stomach turn. The Babylonian industry that grew up around my deified wife converted my secluded, secret world into a village square, one with me standing pilloried at its center, naked and on show for a peanut-crunching, sensation-hungry public.

I burned her last journal after her death, afraid the children would one day see it, and another journal was lost during the numerous moves, just as so much else vanished—thanks to my absentminded distraction— or was stolen by one of the countless visitors to Court Green. Even the signatures she'd written in her books, making them her inalienable property, were either cut or torn out.

The burned journal was a betrayal of our marriage, a dismal tirade with no room for others, for the children, for our love. Everything that made her gentle and lovely—her humor, shyness, perseverance, thoughtfulness, and devotion—was absent. The cobalt blue of her aura was simply overwhelmed by the furious red of her blood. She was governed during the last months of her life by the tyrants of a fundamentalism whose only values were absolute and extreme: black or white, all or nothing, victory or defeat. The fate reserved for all the players in her drama also befell me: as soon as she could no longer worship a person, she hated them—with the same fiery passion with which she'd lauded them. She knew no other way of keeping love alive. The journal's only real message, running throughout all the unrelenting spitefulness, was that she didn't want to go on living unless I went back to her.

Partly out of fear of becoming entangled again in an all-absorbing mar-riage, partly out of my loyalty and love for my one and only bride, I could never give my black muse the certainty she longed for. Once back at Court Green, I tried to live with the heroic indifference an animal feels toward its own destiny, shielded the children as much as I could from an unbearable truth, took my increasingly dependent par-ents under my roof, endured with resignation their tacit disapproval of my wanton existence, handled my wife's literary legacy with the aid of my repatriated sister, had other women besides my relationship with my beloved, and sought out, as often as I could, a hut in the orchard or the silent riverbanks to escape the squawking tribe which—against my will—had elected me chief. One day, while searching for a kindred spirit, I read Arthur Miller's *After the Fall*, a play in which he tried to work through Marilyn Monroe's suicide. When I stumbled across the line about a suicide killing two, I knew he was right.

Seven years after we met, my tormented Lilith made the ultimate attempt to become my wife's equal by not only copying her death, but surpassing it. On March 23, 1969, she put her head in the oven and gassed both herself and our daughter, Shura, just four years old. In death my wife proved to be a more dangerous rival—both as my Eurydice and as a literary artifact—than she could ever be in life. With its macabre eye for detail, history had repeated itself in seven years to forcibly drive something home to me, the stubborn dreamer. When that didn't work, it robbed me yet again of the woman I loved, doubled my punishment by taking my youngest daughter, and three months later, carried off my mother.

As she had anticipated during her life, my Lilith became little more than a footnote in our history, an apocryphal status that also made her posthumously the exile she'd always been. With their literary banishment, the biographers and scribes imitated my own lack of courage and decisiveness in recognizing her.

I didn't have it in me.

I loved her as the first among equals, with the same inconsistency with which I loved all the other women after the death of my bride, as a passerby who at any moment—without explanation or apology—could vanish. In my elusiveness I became the inseparable spouse of a dead loved one, and, with a fatalistic nonchalance, I was sure I was crushing my soul with my licentious existence. The only things that kept me grounded were caring for my children and poetry.

Having been struck dumb for three years, I had started writing a series of epic poems about a crow, but that came to a sudden halt. The crow flew away, and I ran from the resurrected demons into the thorny undergrowth of contemplative prose. Dismembered by an explosion of pain, I once again needed a few years to find my way back to poetry, but even then I wrote about everything except the thing I needed to face in order to heal and to rediscover my real self.

After the suicide of my black muse, I became convinced the gods had it in for me. I was one of the damned, wandering among the shades and infecting all the women in his life with the melancholy darkness that destroys them but gives him a tragic joy. A year and a half after her death, I married a young woman from the land of my youth, a farmer's daughter rooted in the soil, with no literary aspirations, depression, or death wish, a woman who saved the children and me, and not the other way around. She could understand me because she understood the foxes, didn't chain me up like a watchdog, let me go when I strayed.

She waited until I came back. And I always did.

Frieda and Nicholas grew up and emigrated to deserted regions at the edge of the world, bomb shelters where they could protect themselves from the cult surrounding a mother everyone seemed to know, but for whom they cherished no memory at all.

I hardly considered the epistolary poems I had addressed to my wife these past thirty years to be poetry. I felt they were too intimate, too raw, too unpolished, and too private to publish during my lifetime. I thought the search for the truth behind her story, the meaning of mine, was something between her and me.

Until I became ill.

Because of my aversion to confessional, autobiographical literature, my diabolical fear of the purely personal, and my rigid opinions about what true poetry is, until the end of my life I blocked my own absolution.

It was the publication, not the writing, of *Birthday Letters* that set me free. The only way I could be reunited with my bride, pull her back from the underworld, and walk with her toward the sun, was to unveil the first-person singular which I had hidden behind my mask of metaphor or analogy. After her death, the cocoon of the false self I had tried so hard to free her from during our marriage became my own cage, and I kept the fox—which in my dreams leapt against the reinforced glass of my cell—at bay for years. My bride had been dragged away by bloodhounds and devoured, the story of our love taken over and mutilated, and I was too proud and too ashamed to be part of the publishing mob I morally abhorred, and who had continually thwarted my personal processing of the tragedy.

Until Death came so close I could hear him breathing. He bent over me and whispered with my bride's voice that the dramatis personae in our inner world have always striven to be known and heard by others. And I, so long the enemy of the most revealing word in the English language, poured my leaden soul into that slender figure, followed her outside, and I said it, I.

AFTERWORD

Ted Hughes died of a heart attack on October 28, 1998. For the previous year and a half, he'd been receiving treatment for bowel cancer, an illness he'd kept hidden from those around him. On May 13, 1999, Hughes, who in 1984 had been appointed poet laureate of the United Kingdom, was commemorated at Westminster Abbey in London. Queen Elizabeth and Prince Charles were in attendance. In his speech, friend and poet Seamus Heaney said that no death outside his own family had left him as bereft as the death of his friend Ted Hughes, and he went on to describe him as a fortress of tenderheartedness and strength. Frieda Hughes is a poet and painter. She emigrated to Australia but returned to the United Kingdom when her father became ill. Nicholas Farrar Hughes committed suicide at his home in Alaska on March 16, 2009.

AUTHOR'S NOTE

In writing this novel, I drew primarily on the eighty-eight poems in *Birthday Letters*, the collection of Ted Hughes's poems that was published ten months before he died. Some other collections from his extensive body of poetry, such as *Crow: From the Life and Songs of the Crow* (1970), *Capriccio* (1990), and *Howls and Whispers* (1998), were also important to *Your Story, My Story*. A portion of his archives—donated to Emory University in Atlanta, Georgia—was made available to the public in 2000. I derived the depiction of the last meeting between Ted Hughes and Sylvia Plath from his unpublished poem "Last Letter," which was uncovered at that time. Ted Hughes's letters, essays, adaptations, translations, and especially his introductions and comments for the various publications of Sylvia Plath's work were indispensable, as were the critical studies of his work, particularly those of Keith Sagar, Ann Skea, and Diane Middlebrook. At the time this novel was written, there was only one biography of Hughes: *Ted Hughes: The Life of a Poet* (2001) by Elaine Feinstein. The biography *Lover of Unreason: Assia Wevill, Sylvia Plath's Rival and Ted Hughes' Doomed Love*, written by Yehuda Koren and Eilat Negev, was published in 2008.

Beyond Sylvia Plath's poems, stories, journals, and letters, I limited myself to the innumerable biographies and scholarly studies of Plath and her work that appeared prior to Ted Hughes's death and that may have had an influence on his life.

There is a sealed box in Ted Hughes's archives that he delivered to Emory University in person. That box will remain sealed until 2023.

TRANSLATORS' NOTE

Connie Palmen's *Your Story, My Story* is a closely researched fictional account of the relationship between Ted Hughes and Sylvia Plath. The challenge we faced as translators was in bringing Palmen's prose into English, where the story has already been told countless times in biographies, letters, journals, and poems—many written by Hughes himself. It was clear from the start that Palmen uses this couple's story as a framework to examine her own recurrent themes: the struggle to achieve success as a writer, as well as the tension between imagination and the use of autobiographical experiences in creative writing. What is the effect of fame on those who achieve it? When half of a couple is troubled by mental illness, how much responsibility does the other half bear? Who holds the cards in a relationship? Who is the victim, and who has the upper hand? The puzzle in reading Palmen is understanding why she picked a particular story, and that's where the creativity lies: in her selection of facts, and in the way she expounds her own views through the voice of her characters. In her skillfully crafted prose, every word is weighed and every sentence matters.

Palmen's works are highly autobiographical and grounded in philosophy, with the exception of two books: *Lucifer* (based on a real-life case of suspected murder, a work not yet translated into English that she has described as her Old Testament novel) and *Your Story, My Story* (which she describes as her New Testament or Judas novel). The Judas connection is crucial here, as the Ted Hughes character states from the beginning that the key events in his relationship with Sylvia were set in stone before they ever met. In other words, the trajectory of their marriage was fixed from their first encounter. Does that absolve him of all guilt in this tale? Was he simply an unsuspecting accomplice? Or does this make Sylvia less of a victim? In her novel, Palmen lets the reader decide. Amid all the writing about these famous figures, Connie Palmen saw an aspect of their story that hadn't previously been told, one that required immense delicacy to relate impartially, leaving room for ambiguity in spite of narrating only one side.

Our aim in the English translation was to create a credible voice for Hughes while conveying Palmen's incisive prose and her highly conscious use of vocabulary, with its echoes of Hughes's poems. Although based on true stories about the main characters, this is very much a work of fiction by Connie Palmen, one that builds on her previous works and toward the next. We hope her other books will be made available in English soon.

TRANSLATORS' ACKNOWLEDGMENTS

We were greatly helped in our task by the guidance of our mentor, Michele Hutchison, whose support was generously provided for by the Dutch Foundation for Literature and the Centre of Expertise for Literary Translation (ELV). Jacky-Zoë de Rode's excellent MA thesis, "Writing in the Voice of an English Poet: Challenges of Translating Connie Palmen's *Jij zegt het* into English," was also an indispensable resource, as was a conversation with Arlette Ounanian, the translator of the French edition of this novel. Connie Palmen herself was immensely helpful in answering our questions and commenting on drafts, and Elizabeth DeNoma, Judith Bloch, Erin Cusick, Nanette Bendyna-Schuman, and Lauren Grange each played an essential role in honing the text.

ABOUT THE AUTHOR

Photo © Tessa Posthuma de Boer

Connie Palmen was born in Sint Odiliënberg, the Netherlands, and studied literature and philosophy at the University of Amsterdam. She is the author of *The Laws*, voted the European Novel of the Year and short-listed for the 1996 International IMPAC Dublin Literary Award; *The Friendship*, winner of the AKO Literature Prize; *Lucifer*; and the autobiographical novel *I.M.* Ms. Palmen currently lives in Amsterdam. For more information, please visit www.conniepalmen.nl.

ABOUT THE TRANSLATORS

Photo © 2020 by Lous Scholten van Aschat

Eileen J. Stevens earned her MA in linguistics with a specialization in translation from the University of Amsterdam. Her Dutch-to-English translations include Karin Schacknat's *In and Out of Fashion* and Vera Mertens's *The Concentration Camp*. She is a co-translator of Ineke van Doorn's *Singing from the Inside Out*. A New Jersey native, Eileen worked as a professional violinist for twenty-five years before devoting herself to literary translation. She lives in Amsterdam. For more information, visit www.keyboardtranslations.com.

Photo © 2020 by Anna Asbury

Anna Asbury studied classics and linguistics at Cambridge University before moving to the Netherlands for a PhD at Utrecht University. Her translations include Paul De Grauwe's *The Limits of the Market* and Bastiaan Rijpkema's *Militant Democracy: The Limits of Democratic Tolerance*. She is a co-translator of Koen Vossen's *The Power of Populism* and Fréderike Geerdink's *The Boys Are Dead*. She lives in Cambridge, UK. For more information, please visit www.annaasbury.com.